ABYSSES

THE
SEAGULL
LIBRARY OF
FRENCH
LITERATURE

ABYSSES

(*Last Kingdom III*)

Pascal Quignard

TRANSLATED BY CHRIS TURNER

LONDON NEW YORK CALCUTTA

INSTITUT
FRANÇAIS
INDIA

Liberté · Égalité · Fraternité
RÉPUBLIQUE FRANÇAISE
AMBASSADE DE FRANCE EN INDE

This work is published with the support of
Institut français en Inde – Embassy of France in India

Seagull Books, 2021

Originally published in French as Pascal Quignard, *Abîmes*
© Éditions Grasset & Fasquelle, 2002

First published in English by Seagull Books, 2015
English translation © Chris Turner, 2015

ISBN   978 0 8574 2 870 7

British Library Cataloguing-in-Publication Data
A catalogue record for this book is available from the British Library

Typeset and designed by Seagull Books, Calcutta, India
Printed and bound by WordsWorth India, New Delhi, India

CONTENTS

His silence did not seem a product of adversity. Silence, shadow, ennui and emptiness were connected, for him, with the pleasures to be sought in them. Most often that silence is accompanied by a nudity that is as one with this pure waiting in the half-light. And happiness too. And reading adds another voice to it, an even more singular voice, a voice even stranger than song, a voice maintaining the soul in a total absence of resonance. The reader is like an animal standing on the edge of a lake more ancient than the human voice.

At banquets he was a companion of the utmost goodwill and affability. In the revels following, he was more reserved. He sat apart, uncovered his loins hardly at all, but was stirred and lent the whole of his attention to the indecent goings-on without really becoming involved.

He detested all turbulence.

Violence horrified him.

He avoided the company of men or women who talked too much.

He loved Latin enormously and enjoyed reading most of the authors of the old language that had been written in France in the days of the knights and the courts of Champagne. He wrote down nothing that he hadn't previously read and that hadn't already compelled his reading to echo the rhythms of his breathing.

He wrote that not to stray was a thing beyond his powers.

He wrote that it is difficult to regulate one's desires.

In the fable he composed on the subject of two doves that have tender feelings for each other but are very poor lovers—preferring sentiment to physical pleasure, and tourist-like social curiosity to the asemantic happiness of observing each other in the darkness— an inexplicable lyric impulsion can be felt at the point where the narration is coming to an end, like a wave that has been summoned up by all that has been said, a wave that rolls forward and cannot be held back.

This element of song, which has no more story to tell and has become quite nakedly musical, is so simple that it takes some effort to escape its power and attend to the thoroughly unchristian, primal, sexual, lethal ideas it is conveying.

Then the wave, like every wave in nature, creates the patch of damp, dull sand on which it washes up.

There is no sparkle at that point.

But amid these darker traces something glimmers, or at least lies breathing in its fearsome, tranquil place of rest.

The ringing beauty of the verses spreads a muted light into the world of sound dying there.

It throws back a strange, muffled luminescence;

a pale *golden glow*;

a *dawn at the wrong moment*;

an *untimely glow*.

A *glimmering* one scarcely knows whether to apportion to the night or the day.

*

The evanescent trace of waters which might be said to be *darker* than the night that follows each sunlit period.

Like waters in which we might have dwelt *before we knew the sun*.

I am trying to conjure up a face, the face of a man who began writing in 1640 or, rather, I am speaking of a world that is, as it were, mirrored in flowing water. Not a distorted but a floating world.

A universe just below the water's surface, with the creamy reflection of the sun.

If one gazes at one's reflection beside the shore,

It isn't oneself one sees

One sees only an image

Which endlessly returns.

*

The famous line of verse describing the temporality that divides the tasks of human beings, the division of time's flows that dislodged them from the moment and wrested them from the animal power of its ecstasy— *Le mal est que dans l'an s'entremeslent des jours* [The unfortunate thing is that, in the year, days are intermingled]—turns out to be a correction at the proof stage dating from 1678.

Jean de la Fontaine noted the change on a piece of card slipped in between the pages.

I went and examined these proofs in the Reserve Section of the old French National Library which was situated, last century, on the rue de Richelieu in Paris' Second Arrondissement.

We shall never again go to refresh our energies— or to read—in that dull yet clamorous atmosphere, in that dimly lit reading room looking out onto a square.

In those days and in that place they had kept the first printed copies which read: '*Il s'entremesle certains jours . . .*'

A little line of no value—or, at least, of scarcely more value than what I can say in memory of that highly unpredictable art.

*

There's a place I love far from the world, a place I lived in before the first eighteen months of my childhood, before the ivy-covered wall and the walnut trees, the bramble bushes and the ditches beside the river Iton. A place in the world where the water is so clear that there are no reflections. I don't know where that place is now or that sort of stream I seem to have known on earth. It was perhaps, if it was on earth, inside my mother, behind her unseen sex, in the shadows harboured there. It is perhaps quite simply a place, a shabby place, a tiny place—that thing I call the Erstwhile. They say that in his swimming pool up on the rock of Capri, the emperor Claudius would repeat a Greek phrase he remembered from a tragedy by Euripides. 'There is no human dominion,' he would recite. 'Above me I see only seabirds.'

They say that President Azaña, dying in Andorra, turned his face to the members of his close circle and mumbled: 'What was that country called? You know, that country that once existed? That country I was president of? I don't remember any more . . .'

The telephone rang. I leant over. I saw the cable that ran along the skirting board and the plug located between door and sofa. I got up, went towards the door, crouched down and pulled out the plug.

The ringing stopped abruptly.

I sat down on the floor, rubbing my hands with satisfaction.

'But . . . this isn't *your* house!' she said.

I thought for a moment, then answered, 'No.'

'What gives you the right to unplug my telephone?'

'The noise.'

She was smoking a cigarette that she held between her cupped hands.

I watched the smoke float up into the gaps just discernible between the thin, white joints of her fingers.

CHAPTER 3

The earth's axis of rotation runs through the polar regions. The sun's rays strike these obliquely. The quantity of heat received is proportional to the angle at which the rays reach their surface. As a child, I got supplies of affection from radiators;

from Godin stoves;

from standard lamps;

from electric sockets;

from pocket torches.

Sometimes there were sudden bright intervals between showers that made their way along the quays in the harbour, sweeping across the blackish lock-gates.

The succession of belts of vegetation and their fauna follow the contours of the mountains.

They too are dependent on the angle of the slope.

How far they advance depends on which way the hillside faces.

For this reason, the highest forests are in dark shadow.

*

Some electric fish can give off up to 550 volts. The electrical field that silently surrounds them is *the ancestor of eyesight*.

*

Matter, as it explodes in space, fuses and subsides again. Either as comet or as planet. There is little difference between repetition and degradation.

Then, in the living world, birth and old age become disconnected.

And later, in the human world, adolescence and obsolescence seem ranged against each other as opposite poles. But at their source sex and death formed one single action, as is betrayed in the identical moaning associated with them.

These two sources that I place at the origin of time aren't opposed diachronically.

It's the same volcano—it's just a question of spurting forth.

On the temporal horizon, death and sexuality are the two faces of the single god Janus who is constantly rejuvenating himself in human communities and who is named January.

What is cleared out and stunted by death and winter is renewed with ever greater brilliance and in ever greater profusion by childbirth and spring.

Along the towpath of the river Yonne, I deadhead the flowers and cut back their little stems to make them grow more profusely.

They accumulate, proliferate, unfurl, peep open, take on colour.

The thinkers of ancient Japan were of the view that, as time passes, as the numbers of the dead increase, as the host of lives grows in number, as time is stored up and becomes fertile, the spring that bursts out is newer and newer, the newness surrounding us denser and denser.

*

Desire takes us out of ourselves. It takes us out of the *here* of space. It takes us out of the *idem* of the sexed body.

Two fragments of time suddenly polarize, lending ecstatic intensity to the relationship.

In both cases, the polarity is intensified to the point of creating an axis. That axis and that tension provide an orientation. Desire reaches out and breaks down the wall of time by a sudden reciprocity (for time, being irreversible, fractures when suddenly reversed).

Each pole intensifies so strangely.

This is the sexual *co-ire*.

Ire in Latin means go. Loving consists in a momentary co-errancy.

A momentary togetherness.

A momentary wondrous togetherness. A moment that bursts forth and subsides again. They whisper. They lock fingers more tightly than ever they merge their bodies.

Language is the site where speakers are interchangeable. Where differences are relinquished, where sexual polarization is relinquished. Language is the field where polarization is depolarized, where sexes are forgotten, where humans engage in exchange. The lifelong *I* that we exchange in language isn't sexed.

Then desire is reborn. Time is reborn. The spring is reborn. Separation is reborn. Difference is reborn.

*

All ancient societies believed it was down to them to take temporal, celestial, animal, natural, sexual flows and redirect them magnetically to their advantage. To siphon off the flow of the past—that was what political economy consisted in. The historiography the first cities appended to themselves did just that—an agglutinating, magical, deceptive, horrendously retroactive rhetoric took hostage the earliest days, the 'springtime', the days of birth and fecundity, so as to bring them back again.

At its source, history was *a decoy set to catch time*.

*

The peculiar impression of 'coming back down to earth' probably echoes the initial experience of birth through which a living creature leaves one world for another.

A new distension at the source of time arises from language, which rends the given and opposes term for term everything it can distinguish within it—that is to say, everything it hallucinates as lost, desirable, lacking or as a source of hunger.

Finally, the last shift is a consequence of language—it is the shift individual death introduces into human experience (that is to say, death that is named, since there is no such thing as individual death until there is an individual who identifies himself as himself on the basis of a proper name that sets him over against other named identities). A black sun is added to the light. A world that is no more bestows an intimate name beyond the point of its own passing. A little abyss.

CHAPTER 4

Ut sol

Ovid described female pleasure. *Adspicies oculos tremulo fulgore micantes ut sol a liquida saepe refulgent aqua.* As she climaxes, the eyes of a woman sparkle with a brilliance that shimmers like the sun's rays reflected in clear water.

On top of this soft, liquid luminosity come plaints.

Then a muttering.

Then moans.[1]

The vision of ecstatic joy presents itself as a reflection on the surface of 'flowing water' (*liquida aqua*).

A tiny invisible thunderbolt that sends a tremor into the eyes of the women who acquiesce in voluptuous sensuality.

Ovid's thinking here is close to that of Spinoza, for whom sexual pleasure is not joy experienced directly but the reflection of a greater joy. Of a volcanic onto-logical joy. A joy of beings in being. *Ut sol*: like the sun pouring forth its rays—this is the way musicians think. A joy worthy of the radiant sun. A natural joy, but one that pre-dates nature's invention of animal sexuality—a joy of the Erstwhile. A solar joy on which the earth has drawn, on which life has drawn. An expansive joy of which we are merely the reflection. The reflection of a brilliance quivering beneath the mass of water that was there before us. An abyssal, distant, ancient, fragile reflection, never linguistic, unless mutely so.

CHAPTER 5

Suddenly my breathing stopped. Someone behind me was talking about Marthe.

I had sufficient resolve not to turn around. I stood stock-still. Pretending my attention was elsewhere, I began to eavesdrop frantically on what was being said behind my back.

There is something phobic in language as soon as a person you once loved is involved. The ear acquires a sudden sharpness and you return to levels of attention achieved only by animals. The whole body tenses.

From the depths of the body the voice itself rises in register, recovering something of its childish nature.

Your little acts of cunning become difficult to control.

You think you've cleverly dropped a—hopefully anodyne—question into the conversation, but it carries such anxiety about what has become of your former loved one that it wholly gives the game away.

Your voice lowers.

Your breathing grows husky.

A certain slowness creeps into your manner of expression, a more meticulous precision, as though a remnant of attraction forever survived the lost intimacy, the broken bonds and the ignorance of the months or years that now separate you from the moment of break-up or bereavement.

Your words brush against a self-interested, zoological, naked, intimate, possessive zone that has remained intact deep within you, despite the time that has passed and is lost for ever.

This fissure or abyss reopened by the words you are straining to hear is a sick curiosity.

Forever sick.

Forever sick because it was wounded deeply, precisely to the extent that it gave itself wholly, with the whole body, spontaneously and irresistibly.

Sick to death unto death because it had given everything, including even its fear, its vision, its exposure, its shame.

*

This is how a whole stretch of country, *a heathland of passion open to every wind* and to every indiscretion extends behind you, immense and whispering, while you pretend your ears are closed.

There's an attention here that's involuntary.

In reality, nothing can silence the jealousy you still feel towards the other's body, though you have, in fact, relinquished it.

Nothing diminishes the extraordinary calmness that accompanies this attentiveness, which is that of the knight errant advancing amid the hawthorn bushes in the pale air.

It is an alerting of the ineradicable. I spoke about Marthe in *Le Salon du Wurtemberg*. I loved her in 1977.

CHAPTER 6

Once again the Württemberg landscape was magnificent. The snow had stopped falling. The sky was white. The hills white, the trees white.

CHAPTER 7

The Seasons and the Sentences[2]

From the very first brush-stroke, figure and ground emerge together.

And they stand opposed as two poles.

In active predation, in the springing of carnivores as they leap on their prey—in the projection of all those beings projecting themselves onto their opposite pole— the background and the admirable body that moves and stands out against it are suddenly uncoupled.

Hunting is the background of art.

Lying in wait the background of contemplation.

Hunger the background of desire.

Carnivorousness the background of admiration.

Time was first conceived as predation. Beings as its prey.

*

The source of history—nycthemeral periodicity is gradually ennobled into seasonal periodicity.

A regularity encompassed the rhythm of the group in its own presence to itself.

In Latin, the word presence means 'bringing closer'. The times when individuals are brought closer within groups are called festivals. The group, rending the rent between day and night into that of the solstices, stretched things to a point where the roles created were parcelled out into a celestial, annual, communal journey.

*

Photophores are bearers of light, *doryphores*—the French word for Colorado beetles—bearers of a spear [*doru*] and egophores are bearers of the little word 'I'.

The little word 'I', which speakers place at the source of their cries and to which gradually they lend credence, from which they hope for a little clarity, in which they dream of valour.

With the little word 'I', the linguistic sentence founds a reciprocal relation between speaker and addressee.

The egophores who toss involuntary natural language to one another in the form of dialogue receive it in their bodies in the form of an echo of the acquired 'national' language (consciousness). Each time they address one another, they ground anew the possibility of human society (that is to say, reciprocity, war, religion, envy).

In passing on the baton of the little word 'I', they annihilate one another mutually (they exchange one another).

A sentence immediately creates a world along two axes which recast the environment and transfigure sexuality.

The sentence founds another relation than the sexual. The sexual relation does not oppose, it does not polarize—it differentiates. The Latin word *sexus* means 'separation'.

The linguistic relation, rending asunder for ever the referencing and the referenced, sets up an axis between humanity and the earth which it immediately ranges against each other. An axis that runs from language to nature, from the chronological to the timeless, from the discontinuous to the continuous, from the subject to the thing-in-itself, from the horizon of the world to the invisible source of the origin.

The egophores in their dialogue are at the outer limit of the predatory face-off they imitate. They stand on the frontier of the envious opposition or lethal hostility they generate by speaking, listening, obeying. Their world is on the edge of an abyssal line.

The acquisition of the reciprocal relation is itself reciprocal (fusional, contemporaneous), like the bond between mother and child.

The acquisition of the second axis is non-reciprocal (asynchronous, historical), like the father–son connection (the unconnectedness of the two pieces—never to be joined again—which form the symbol, the inaccessible citeriority of the past and its sempiternal domination of new arrivals in their matter, form, gender, faces, expressions and relations).

Face-off between World and Meaning, Being and Time.

*

The two temporal poles that arise with Man (who emerges before the inner vocalization of acquired language in the form of personal consciousness) configure things in each language along lines specific to each language but they also extend that configuration into all social forms.

It is the linguistic formation of words in the natural languages that leaves behind adversation and sexuation and dooms human thought to opposition.

At that point, irreversion and repetition are polarized as *Alter* and *Idem*.

Human societies accentuate them by ritualizing them. Each year, the non-working days recur, the holidays, the holy days. The circular return of Eden, of the Erstwhile, of births, of the anniversaries of births, of the initiations that reiterate them.

The Circle that is dispersed along time's arrow stands over against the haunting uterine point. An invisible Here that becomes There where we were. A non-time that haunts time. A Here that traverses the There. A Here which, like mysterious shifting sands in which all identity is lost, beckons human beings into a depressive state.

*

Signs are dipoles. The earth itself is a dipole running along the axis of rotation on which the magnetic North coincides with the geographic. Volcanoes are the active memories of this magnetization, in the same way as nervous breakdowns, the abysses of depression, return all along the linguistic axis.

*

It is my contention that time doesn't have three dimensions. It is just this beating, this to-and-fro. It is simply this non-oriented rending.

What remains of the essence of primal time in human beings is this two-phase beat comprising the lost and the imminent.

Croce said: 'History is always contemporary history.'

The linguistic construction of the presence of the past is always contemporary with the irreversible, unorientable, physical erstwhile that flows within it.

Current times are constantly telling themselves a story—they are orienting their lost element (orienting what cannot be oriented, what is disoriented). In the USSR, for example, in the middle of last century, the past was completely unpredictable. For fifty years, what had happened in the past changed from one day to the next.

*

Coitus is a dipole. Desire and pleasure are, themselves, distant from each other. In the persons of man and woman, impatience and delay stare each other in the face. Between these poles comes a *lapsing* of time. Saint Jerome's Bible called original sin by the name *lapsus*. In music, that is what we call the *empty bar or measure*.

The beating of time lies at the heart of the coming-together that precedes birth.

*

Social time is neither linear nor cyclical. It is (1) dipolar, like sexuality; (2) oppositive, like the language that makes it possible.

Social time contains the contraries of admonition and transgression, of calm and disturbance, of individualization and communion. The life of each among all is, predominantly, a string of nexuses of rules, studded with moments of disorder. These times of disorder and excitation are the times of bloodletting and rejoicing.

*

Languages are the selectors of time and tenses. They put labels on actions indicating which precedes and which occurs later or concomitantly. We talk of past, future and present, though we might speak of accomplishment and near or distant imminence. This tripartite division is not part of languages themselves. Even less is it part of all the natural human languages which know nothing of it whatever. Things are sorted this way by a mythic selection procedure. If they are sorted into threes, that is because myths, in common with their heroes, are fond of ordeals that come in threes, like the families of viviparous creatures. But the suspense this progression entails has to do with time itself—with captivating, pre-linguistic time that operates by twos, as languages do. Temporality is more primal than the languages that label it or the myths that set out in search of it. The acquisition of these things in childhood fixes these prior divisions in the child's mind, concealing their nature beneath a fanatical formula, ritual obedience and obsessive internalization. However, just as these forms cannot be deduced from time itself, so too these labels cannot be distinguished from the languages that establish them and enable us to think in terms of them.

*

The origin of the future was the dream image. Then the hallucinatory image. Then a grief-stricken one. There are three worlds: the predators, the prey and the dead. The three houses of the soul correspond to the three worlds of the Siberian shamans. In the French folk song, Cadet Rousselle at Auxerre has three houses.

If we term what dates from cave-dwelling times antiquated and are intent on eliminating its return, then concupiscence, shame, death, sexuality, anxiety, language, fear, the voice, envy, vision, gravity, hunger and joy have to be proscribed.

The emperor Augustus was born under the consulate of Cicero in 63 BCE, on the ninth day before the calends of October, before dawn, in the cellar of his house, in the part of the Palatine called At the Oxheads (*Ad capitula Bubula*).

Oxen that still had quite a bit of the auroch in them.

A fifty-six-year reign, forty-four of them years of solitary power.

He always wore a hunting knife in his belt.

He used to say all the time, in Greek, *Speude bradeos*, which in English means 'Make haste slowly.'

In Latin: *Festina lente*.

The hieroglyph on coins and arches that commemorates him is the dolphin and anchor.

An extraordinary proverb, after the fashion of *impossibilia*, in that in two words it expresses human time, that mixture of thrust and return, of leaping above the waves and anchorage at the bottom of the sea, of event and repetition, of *morsus* [bite] and remorse, of the erstwhile and the now.

Suetonius adds that the phrase suggesting that an item of business or a decision be put off to the Greek Calends (*ad Kal. Graecas*—that is to say, to the calends that do not exist—*sine die*) is an expression also said to have been invented by the emperor Augustus.

So he would sit down.

The emperor was waiting for the lost object, with his hand on his hunting knife.

Then with his hand on everything that looked like a hunting knife. This is the link between *stylus* and *stylo* [pen].

CHAPTER 10

Treatise on Antiquaries

We should defend antiquaries and see them as the opposite of historians.

It's about emphasizing the virtues of anecdotists and their harvest of miscellaneous events, in contrast to concealment and propaganda.

In the death that repetition repeats to the point of oblivion, we should prefer the collector of beauty (current piety towards what was invisible) to the statesman who spins horrors and howls of pain to his advantage as a way of gaining control, to the journalist paid by one of the rival pressure groups to impose the will to power of his paymasters, to the historian bankrolled by the state to simplify and dress up what has been, and to the philosopher paid by the state to provide it with justification, direction, meaning and value.

*

It is often said that admiration for what is old is a recent passion. This is contradicted by examples from the past. The taste for the old is a luxury that has always characterized power in human societies. Old drugs, old skulls, old wine, old totems, old manuscripts, old weapons, old relics—all these objects that conduct the act of foundation as though it were an electric current—make that act anew each time as the Before of what is.

In these different objects it is the origin that is venerated.

There are pages written in Rome on antiquaries that enchant by the diversity and folly of the obsessions they indicate. It was only as a result of the imperatives of capitalist industry and the Christian religion that the old came to be seen as the decrepit, the unwieldy, the dirty, the heathen, the contagious, the dispensable, the disgusting.

*

The antiquary detests the completed—he loves what is before birth. He too seeks to seize on that which comes before any springtime. He wants to pre-empt the de-synchronization of his words from his senses, of his sensations from his emergence into the atmosphere.

He weaves dreams around his conception.

What was inaccessible to the existence of his own body obsesses him.

I define beauty as piety towards what was invisible at birth. A vast diptych: (1) the first uterine world; (2) the sexual world that precedes the uterine world and gives it life.

Every work [*oeuvre*] is a Renascence because even life precedes birth, from which point it begins again.

*

A ceaseless reversal of polarities between bipoles means that the heroism or penchant for suicide of the ancient Japanese or the ancient Romans may make a comeback among modern peoples (Romantics, terrorists, the religious), though with the opposite meaning.

The most puritanical Christian maxims are suddenly reversed.

Memento mori turns around into *Memento vivere*.

Inversion dominates folktales, which are merely language driven to excess that has suddenly fallen under the dominion of dreams. The Renaissance was stirred up by the excessive images of the Christian mysticism of the late Middle Ages which was suddenly used in *a way that deliberately misconstrued it.*

*

33

The only true antiquity in us is birth. It is through birth that what precedes it surges up within us while at the same time being lost.

Many animals collect objects.

They are their nests.

The nest is the place of birth.

The only object we are really looking for, in all the objects we accumulate, is lost.

*

On the desire to return underground. To go back to the abyss. To die (or, rather, to be buried).

It is possible that the desire among viviparous creatures to go back under the earth is connected exclusively with regret. It is the desire to fall back—in a state of total nakedness—into the darkness of the womb. (To hide behind something of the order of a dark, protective anteriority. In their boldness in penetrating abysses and mountain caves, the most ancient human beings shared in this desire to go back under the earth and return to the semi-darkness particular to the former foetuses that they, like we, were.)

Corollary: an antiquary should not light too brightly the place where he lays out his treasures for sale.

*

The antiquaries who abounded in ancient Rome claimed to be specialists in the Golden Age. Post-religious piety gives birth to the cult of ancient times. The first meaning of *archaiologia* refers to the fact of choosing an ancient subject.

Once upon a time, there *was*.

The hero is linked to the Erstwhile because he is tasked with founding the Present.

In all the world's stories, heroes found cities, arts, customs, languages, instruments, recipes.

*

Heroes provide antiquaries with material.

*

Euctus' list.

Euctus, long before Jesus' time, collected ancient pottery in the land of Saguntum.

He would show people a cup from which Laomedon had drunk.

An oil lamp that had been used by Homer.

Dido's black patera from Bitias' banquet.

CHAPTER 11

Varro

Varro was born in 640. He died *prope nonagenarius* (almost in his nineties) in the Roman year 728. He was ten years older than Cicero or Pompey, who were his friends, and whom he survived by many years. His curiosity was indefatigable. He was the second archaeologist, Stilo having been the first.[3] The word used in those days was antiquary. Literally, the man obsessed with what was before (*ante*).

Cicero wrote of him, in Greek, that he was a terrifying man (*deinos anèr*).

Tall, stern, thin, uncouth, irascible, loud-mouthed, gloomy.

*

Cicero said of reading that it was the food of exile.

Varro retorted that it was the homeland.

*

Varro wrote: 'Legendo atque scribendo vitam procud-ito' (It is by reading and writing that one forges one's life like iron).

*

Varro wrote that scrolls had provided his life with a *medicinam perpetuam* (a definitive cure).

He grew old in his study, close by his aviary.

*

Under the principate of Augustus, though still alive, he was almost a ghost.

Pliny reports that the emperor Augustus showed him great consideration, despite his reprimands, the harshness of his character and his unpredictable fits of anger, telling those who were astonished by this: 'In binding Varro to me, I bind the past.'

At the age of eighty-seven, the scholar was still publishing his four annual volumes.

*

In his will he requested that he be buried like the Pythagoreans, in a brick coffin with *black poplar leaves.*

CHAPTER 12

Nostalgia

The word nostalgia was coined by a physician from Mulhouse called Hofer. The invention took place in 1678. Dr Hofer was trying to find a name to define an illness affecting mercenaries, particularly those who were natives of Switzerland.

Suddenly, without even seeking to desert from the companies in which they had enlisted, these Swiss—foot-soldiers and officers alike—were pining to death in sorrowful longing for their Alpine pastures.

They wept.

When they talked, they reminisced endlessly about the ways of their childhood.

They hanged themselves from the branches of the trees, with the names of their sheepdogs on their lips.

Doctor Hofer searched in his Greek dictionary for the word for return, then took from it also the term for suffering. Combining *nostos* and *algos,* he made nostalgia.

In crafting this word in 1678, he gave a name to the sickness of the baroque age.

*

The pain of irreversibility which, out of what was, wrests the *It was*.

Irreversibility, which deprives us absolutely of the gaze that prevailed.

Which no longer has the accented hum of the old language in its ears. Which frees us from the natural envelope of unseasonable, restless, bounding childhood—a childhood that is *rudis, animalis*. Which knows nothing of the as yet very vague social obedience demanded of infants.

*

Nostalgia is a structure of human time that brings to mind the solstice in the heavens.

*

The first source of time invented in the emotions of human beings ranged against nature takes elliptical or circular form—it is return. It is spring coming back, the return of the sun with the new day and the return of the sun over the year, the return of the night stars, the return of plants after winter, the return of animals and humans after they have hunted (after they have been hunted).

Survival means the poignant return of the spring.

It means reaching the following spring.

The sickness from that failed return is primal. The pain of it throws the psyche into panic in its desire to re-find the old home and its familiar faces. This is the malady of Ulysses, the malady of the hunters who have strayed far from the hearth and the circle of women, the malady of heroes.

*

Stronger than everything, it would seem, is the attraction of the Erstwhile in the pull one may feel towards one's native land.

Euripides the Tragedian adds categorically: 'Whoever denies this is playing with words and his thinking belies him.'

It is, rather, his body that belies him.

Moreover, it is not land that is at issue here.

The Tragedian is referring to authentic thought, the thinking that experienced things *before* the cranium was conquered by the national language. He is referring to infant thought. He is referring to *continuous desire*. As soon as it is continuous, it is regressive.

Regret for a place that lies inside a belly, not on a patch of land.

*

Mourning is felt as soon as, within the natal, the nascent evaporates.

A growing light stagnates.

Then the discovery of the light is tarnished.

*

Pierre Nicole wrote: 'The past is a bottomless abysm which swallows all transient things; and the future another abysm impenetrable to us; the one flows continually into the other; the future discharges itself into the past by flowing through the present; we are placed between these two abysms and we feel it; for we feel the flow of the future into the past; this sensation creates the present above the abysm.'

Abyss in Greek means bottomless, just as aorist means limitless.

A-byssos of time.

To be very precise, we call the deepest places in the oceans abysses *as soon as the light of the sun no longer reaches them.*

*

The hallucinatory return of the experience of satisfaction is the first psychical activity.

Dreaming precedes it, hallucinating as it does those beings whose bodies are absent, and doing so as part of an involuntary confusion.

This is how *nostos* is at the base of the psyche.

The malady ensuing from the impossible return of the lost—nostalgia—is the first vice of thought, alongside the partiality for language.

Though we ought to suggest that the acquisition of natural language is itself perhaps just an illness revolving around the return of the lost element, since the aim is to bring back the first voice—the mother's voice—just as it was, inside oneself, and to do so at a point when one can no longer be inside the maternal flesh itself and wholly exposed to its accents—and to an immediate stream of food.

An endless, inexhaustible past is thus defined within the human being, taking as its starting point the mother and her voice, heard once upon a time in the distance.

The simple past of the mother tongue which answers to the abyss constituted by the displacement of birth.

*

A-patridity—statelessness—answers to the aorist which answers to the abyss.

Statelessness in human beings derives from the loss of the first viviparous world. Those being born suddenly draw breath, feeling nostalgia for an unfindable internal place. They may *dream of* an autochthony that has no existence but they will never be born *from the earth* on to which they fell, after having lived already—sheltered by a womb of skin—within the interiority of a distant, incomprehensible voice. The idea of fatherland is a later one (90,000 years of humanity separate humanity from the idea of a sedentary way of life which was also, later, copied from the ancestors via their tombs, grouped together as other-worldly cities set down in space).

We were hunters and wanderers for millennia before we dug into the earth as farmers and saw our buried fathers there because that was where we had interred them.

*

In Greek, *noesis* and *nostos* are from the same root. To think is to regret. To regret is to see what is not before our eyes. It is hunger hallucinating what it lacks. It is the widower seeing the face of the wife he has lost. It is the freezing individual awaiting the sun. Thinking, desiring and dreaming are based on a coming that doesn't stop, a *subvenire* that persists beneath the *venire* within everything that happens in the Advent. An Erstwhile is the foundation of these. The lost body and the Erstwhile are very much akin. In the first romance ever written in this world, when King Gilgamesh no longer knows what to do, when he has to find a stratagem or ruse to extricate himself from a perilous situation, a state of imminent danger, he tells Enkidu that he is going to sleep, so as to have a dream which will show the goal to be achieved—and how to achieve it—as soon as he has repeated it to him in the form of language.

*

No psychical life can be born without the aid of another, prior psychical life. Before his arrival, an ancestral pre-life dreams for the new arrival the existence of a psychic life comparable to its own. It is in this way that there is a new-coming of the Erstwhile that rises up from the Erstwhile.

*

Such is the Erstwhile: What we have forgotten doesn't forget us. Every baby who is born has already emigrated.

CHAPTER 13

He liked to play old men. He also liked to take the part of spectres. If there was the role of a ghost in a play, the members of the troupe would say, 'That's for Shakespeare.'

CHAPTER 14

Low C

One day when a monk called Paul at Monte Cassino was due to sing, his voice failed him. So he knelt to pray, and Saint John the Baptist granted him permission to invent low C.

His lips parted.

His voice rose up, if we can speak of rising up where puffing and groaning is concerned.

All the monks began to weep with sorrow at the sound of such a deep bass voice that it seemed to come from the Underworld.

*

After the service the monk Paul thanked John the Baptist.

But it wasn't for Saint John the Baptist that he ordered nine Masses.

It was Saint Zacharias, rather, that he turned to. For Zacharias was the saint to whom children whose voices had broken prayed for their lost voices. Now, the voice that had been given to the monk Paul was darker in tone. This is why all professional singers venerate Saint Zacharias.

Even today, they light a candle to his statue when they wish to be sure of their voices for an upcoming concert.

CHAPTER 15

I am thinking of my father. We were living at Bergheim. He was an organist. By night we fished, using a mirror, on the Jagst or the Avre. I can't precisely remember the name of the river that flowed past the bottom of the hill. I'm making the hill up but plucking the riverbank from memory. The water bailiff prepared the flat boat beside the bank. He placed a dark lantern (later he replaced the lantern with a small stove) in the prow of the boat. A circular tin mirror, made in Nuremberg, arranged above the lantern, reflected the flame down into the abyss. These fishing trips were miraculous. In my excitement I couldn't stand still in the reeds, just as I couldn't help stamping my feet with impatience in the organ loft behind the bellows that Herr Geschich trod slowly, amplifying the sound in the direction of God and His Night.

CHAPTER 16

Night is the name I give to the light that's lost in space; the light that dissipates before it reaches human beings.

There is some obscurity about the night sky being so obscure.

If the universe were eternal, then at nightfall the sky would shine with countless billions of stars, resembling a vast canopy that would dazzle the eyes of vertebrates and birds alike.

The night sky is dark *for want of time*.

Since the formation of the first stars in space, light has always lacked the time needed to reach the eyes of the animals that see them.

Darkness is this slowness in space. (Not a slowness in shining out but a slowness in perceiving the immensity that shines out.)

Slowness is space.

Darkness is precisely the name the Bible gives to this *loss over time*. Light lost on the way from far-off regions that the gaze no longer reaches.

Night is merely an infinite light. All light propagating itself in space at a finite velocity is infinitely inaccessible.

The *limes* of the simple past.

Such is the *black night* in the sky.

The sky is bathed in inaccessible light. It is our dark companion. All our companions have a light dusting of stars.

CHAPTER 17

Amaritudo

In sensual delight, the desire to be happy is lost. The more you give yourself over entirely to desire, the more is happiness almost there. You are on the lookout for it and that's precisely where you go wrong. You expect to meet it. You sense its coming. Suddenly, you see it; you expect it even more; it draws nearer; it arrives. As it arrives, it destroys itself.

This argument enables us to understand those who decide to opt for chastity.

Desire is linked to the immeasurable lost element.

In two ways. (1) Desire is closer to what is lost than—the subsequent—genital pleasure which believes it can gain access to it. (2) You lose desire in sexual climax. That loss, most unpleasant in its consequences, is the very definition of sensual delight.

*

Pleasure means discovering, to your amazement, that desire has been lost without trace; it means detumescence, a lack of excitability, revulsion, weariness, acedia, discomfort, sleep.

Desire is contrary to the puritanical notion of happiness. Lasting desire is cheerfulness mingled with anxiety. True desire isn't out for its own extinction in satisfaction; it is effervescence and disorder; it is closer to the relentlessness of hunger than to peace; everything exacerbates it and builds passionately upon it; for everything, it marks an end to peace; it inflames what it touches and injects life, does violence to its objects and amplifies a future to come which, above all, must not come.

*

Suddenly the strength of an attachment no longer depends on any circumstance. The mind is suddenly scrambled by a pipe-dream. The body tenses for something or other which never happens.

*

In the case of the happy person, hope has deserted him, his life is almost dead, desire is lost. He doesn't even dream, he has gone off into the night, *he sleeps too deeply to dream.*

CHAPTER 18

It is pleasant to abandon.

To abandon is to depart, to leave.

One should always leave.

Pleasure is: I am leaving.

CHAPTER 19

Some events in life are like storms descending on us.
You take to your heels across plain or moorland. You're
a long way from anywhere. There's not a clump of trees
to be seen. No ditch beside the fields. No overhanging
rock, no wreck of an abandoned car that could offer
cover. The clouds scud by above. They are black. They
are black as blocks of anthracite. The clouds glisten and
touch the trees; suddenly, the hail begins to crackle.
These little stones falling from the sky bounce up all
around you. You run. You are being stoned by the sky.
You run without rhyme or reason. You cover your head
with your arm, your hand. The rain goes straight
through your clothing. You know there's nothing to be
done. You know that even if you didn't make so much
effort, you'd still be as wet. You know all you can do is
stay standing still, or kneel, with your back to the rain
and allow it to soak you through. But you can't. You

run in all directions as though you could escape the hail, avoid the rain, attract the attention of God, the Almighty, so that He might make an exception and exempt you from suffering. I arrived at Seoul airport in 1987 and was met by a tall European woman. She had long blonde hair. She was Italian. Her eyes had a feverish sparkle to them. She apologized for the absence of her husband who had had to go to Pusan and who would be back the next day. We got into a blue four-by-four. We dined on the eighth floor of a tower block, seated on the ground in a traditional restaurant. We had removed our shoes in the entrance-way. Her foot was damp. We drank rice wine. I looked at her toes squeezed tightly together and difficult to distinguish from one another in the transparency of the stocking. The light reflected off the material covering the bones of her knee as though from a mirror. I reached forward and placed my hand there. She carried on talking. I slipped my fingers beneath the hem of her skirt. She carried on talking. My hand began to tremble. Suddenly, she moved rapidly to place the palm of her hand on my sex for a moment, then the hand vanished. We continued to talk but our hands and eyes went on with a life of their own that no longer paid any attention to language. We went somewhere or other.

She was marvellously fragrant. Her body was long. Her breasts were heavy. Her eyes were black. We made love. I fell asleep.

When she woke me, she was quite different. She was sitting on the edge of the bed, dressed in a suit. She had put on make-up. She was shaking me roughly. It was still night.

'Farewell!' she said.

I looked at her. I felt hurt. I was back in the storm again. Such is my life. She was adept, like no other, at the art of disappearing. I handed the taxi driver the address of the hotel where my publisher had booked a room for me. I set to work. I stayed for a month on the Yellow Sea near Seoul. I wrote treatises, and stories of a kind. I saw her again at Lahti, at the meeting that took place in Finland every year. She was with a young red-haired woman.

CHAPTER 20

Bagdemagus, the king of the Underworld, says of the knights errant: 'They are all lost in this quest as though they were *swallowed by an abyss.*'

In Old French, just as *tempore—temps,* time— meant the human, so too *secle—le siècle,* the century— meant the world. Perceval, finding himself engulfed in greater and greater darkness, sits down slowly on the sacred stone. Here is the text itself: 'Then, when he had sat down, the stone split beneath him and cried out in such anguish that it seemed to all who were there that *the century was collapsing into the abyss.*'

As *we* read it, it is the earth that is caving in, but the text of the romance has it right—even in the collapsing earth, it is time that is crumbling like a cliff wall into shapeless infinity.

CHAPTER 21

On Dead Time

'Refractory period' is the name given to the time when, after spending their seed, sexed male animals are not sexually reactive to any approach or excitation.

The sexual refractory period is the basis of social 'dead time' or downtime.

*

List of instances of dead time.

The ghostly time in the aftermath of wars.

The moment of silence that descends upon nature at the end of the day. As shadows fall, birds quit the realm of sound.

The time following congress between mammals.

Coming to a halt after—continuous or forced— cardiac acceleration and breathlessness.

The invention of the sitting position, the—strange—invention of the pulpit or rostrum for human beings, the reading of books.

*

The Italian Renaissance and, subsequently, the French, striving as they did to bring back the pagan past, in opposition to the eschatology of the Christian Middle Ages, wrested time from the power of God.

The magnetic poles reversed, reversal being the mythic process par excellence. It is *re-flexion*. The secular realm became paradise, love became progress and eternity became dead time.

The North and South Poles only truly changed places among the Ideologues, the Encyclopaedists and the Paris Revolutionaries, then among the *industriels* of the First Empire.

But it was during the Renaissance that the magnetic poles of time suddenly switched round.

*

Two madnesses where time is concerned: nostalgia (melancholy, mourning) and eschatology (progress, last judgement). The Before and the After are merely caricature images of Arrives and Passes Away.

*

Piety towards idols, towards gods, towards languages, together with nationalism, are anti-renaissances.

Every revealed religion desires the destruction of all past gods whom it abruptly downgrades. When the prophetic gods faltered and their promises were no longer believed, nations became religions in the mode of futurity.

Nations became the name for religions grown sick with progress.

As it caused the desire for another life within the heavenly city to be abandoned and replaced by the fraternal, national ideal—a thing of conscription, obligation and burial—patriotism supplanted Gallicanism. The sanctification of the land of the fathers replaced the Christians' faith in eternal paradise.

In other words, we can adequately define religions as the nations of the past.

With the mode of futurity defining progress, its advance is a finite conquest over the immediate finite. Progress is bent on putting the past to death, on repelling or devouring its face. The infinite deserts the human head at the time of *progressio*, which is a step-by-step advance, within the now, in the destruction of the finite.

The global industrialized death invented by the wars of the last century became the earthly face of progress.

The step-by-step of ruination.

Advent as the smell of burning humans.

*

In the course of the twentieth century, science cemented the awareness of the end of this world. All humanity's riches, all the elements of global culture, all books and all memories of the human species will be swallowed up.

The earth will burn.

The sun will burn up.

This is the first time in the evolution of the species that its destruction has become certain and that this engulfing of every human monument, this obliteration of every human achievement, this annihilation of every human value have been taken as read.

This is the first time humanity has had the certainty that there will be time after history.

This swallowing without trace means that all our funerary practices are in vain, despite their being inherent to our condition and definitional of our

species: inhumation, desiccation, manducation, ceno-
taphs, etc.

Both the lengthening of historical times, prehistoric periods, terrestrial times and living times, and the
changeable, fragmentary, ephemeral, fortuitous nature
of human experience.

The first time that humanity can no longer entrust
anything of itself to anything.

Neither to the earth (which will disappear).

Nor to the solar system (which will boil).

*

For the first time within time, future-oriented thinking
looks upon the being of the earth as a prospective
nothingness.

*

The war that began on Sunday, 3 September 1939 at
11 o'clock and ended at dawn on 2 September 1945
fractured time. Those who create nowadays are aware
of an irremediable break in the continuity of Western
history. That history is lost.

Humanity is lost.

The fatherland is lost.

Religion is lost.

Tradition is lost.

Now, it is this lost element in the pure state that gives them hope. For what is lost here is the same Lost Element that constitutes the obscure basis of the arts.

Preceding the distant lament that haunts them.

At the source of the—unbelievably renascent—light that is sought and, to some extent, found in them—if only for a brief moment and in flickering mode.

Human time has been returned to its archaic asemia; to its freedom; to its profusion; to its wildness.

*

The incredibly de-ritualized, de-polarized time of the moderns.

Wang Fuzhi wrote: 'All the creatures in the world lend one another mutual support, except human beings.'

The thunder lends support to the lightning just as the ear lends support to the eye. The night lends support to the day so that the seasons may return. The female lends support to the male so that seed may spurt forth. Sexuality lends support to nutrition so that life may increase in volume and fill up space. Death lends support to life so as not to encumber the earth with all the fruits, all the animals and all the human beings that have been conceived since the beginning.

Wang Fuzhi writes: 'But not the wife to the husband. But not the son to the father. But not the disciple to his master. Not the slave to his owner.'

*

Wanderlust. The desire to travel lies elsewhere. Fleeing the *idem*, seeking the *alter*, recovering the lost—no matter the words, no matter the orientation of the verbs.

*

Explosio est pulsio.

A volcano erupts under pressure from the terrestrial core (what I call terrestrial core is the Erstwhile boiling). After the magnetic chamber which formed a reservoir has swollen, its walls suddenly give way. The abrupt de-pressurization causes a mixture of gas and liquid to shoot out of the top. As soon as that has spurted out, the space freed up in the magnetic chamber draws in a new intake of magma which mingles with this mixture, increasing the quantity of the volatile elements of carbon, water and sulphur.

*

We read imaginary stories the same way we bend our ears to those who have returned from distant islands, after spending years there; those who, with their weather-beaten faces and rickety bodies, with their voices lost to some degree for lack of use and grown a little distant from having to stay silent when surrounded by an abstruse, alien tongue, tell us of the customs and cruelties current in those countries to which we shall never travel.

Countries whose very names are more incomprehensible to our tongues than the name of death.

In those cases, what we like isn't so much the story as the reality, the non-finite distance between places and times, the 'ocean' that separates us from them, the boundless 'space' that keeps them from view, the 'abyss' that lands us back forever on the shore. It is this 'distance beyond all hope of being covered' that we are trying to feel as we read. A distance beyond all hope of coverage between what we have known and what we couldn't have experienced. Books develop faculties and ages in our lives that are richer than the freedom of our dreams. In this way, reading helps us more than travel to get to the bottom of the world.

CHAPTER 22

Pisgah

Standing upon Pisgah, Moses gazed upon the land the Everlasting One had not permitted him to enter.

This was the highest point of the Abarim range, Mount Nebo in the land of Moab.

It was there that the Unutterable One told Moses to exult and then to die as he gazed upon Canaan.

Moses who was doomed to the *limes* between land and desert.

To the threshold between dream and reality.

To the frontier between God and vision.

To the one who walked, the Ineffable said:

'Ascende in montem istud Abarim,
in montem Nebo . . .'

Gaze upon the land of Canaan, then die on the mountain.

Your portion is the infinite.

Wandering your resting place.

Your gaze a dizzying one.

CHAPTER 23

Music is the mirror of what is lost. Language is Losing in action. Ecstasy is the unconscious experience of loss itself. Ecstasy goes to the roots of what is torn away. Ecstasies only occur in beings that possess language, since losing consciousness is losing language.

*

Busoni said that you mustn't perform. What you have to do is re-improvise. Only what is in the process of appearing appears. Hands move along the keyboard, but the hands don't matter. It is a question of being born. Our art consists in origins. Beauty is of no consequence. Behind beauty, it is the source you have to get to.

Busoni wrote that the person called the performer must re-establish what the inspiration of the person known as the composer has necessarily lost by putting it down on paper.

*

You don't know what happened if you don't have the narrative. But narratives never correspond to anything. They refer to another kind of action, which is that of language in motion, and that doesn't tally with experience. The situation that presided over the whole set of actions and the consequences they entailed remains unclear—there is no point of view to it; it is inchoate, abyssal, mysterious. You have to come to terms with this dizzying situation, then learn to love it. Reassurance isn't an option. A so-called objective description satisfies only the fanatical believers in language. A dubious, fragmentary account gradually settles into place. Truth does not out.

CHAPTER 24

She rubbed her eyes with the back of her hands.

Her impenetrable half-brown, half-black eyes.

Nothing luminous ever rose to the surface of that water. Nor even furrowed it. For me, that look was—and has remained—depth itself. It is exactly what the ancient Greeks called the abyss.

Animals too have eyes as direct as this, with no hidden thoughts, nothing in the background; infinite eyes, eyes as serious, as straightforward, as attentive, anxious and devouring as hers. She flexed her knees before sitting.

CHAPTER 25

Crows

All the crows in the world are equally black and come from the night that lies beyond the stars.

The men of gold, said Hesiod, didn't experience old age. They simply died overcome by sleep, so fascinated were they by the night, into which they gazed endlessly.

The demon of darkness prowls around on the last nights of the year. This is the so-called old lady. She threatens to swallow everything: beings, the world, time, the dead, the mountains, the sun, dreams. The peepal tree is the trace of the Buddha in this world. It is the tree in whose shade the wisest man experienced ecstasy (the *excessive revelation*) near Gaya on the banks of the Neranjara.

The peepal tree is less than its shadow.

Other holy men say of the Holiest: 'His Trace is all shadow.'

*

The mystery of the invisible rain that we call Dust on the ebony of the piano and the black cases of the violins, violas and cellos in the little house I had set aside for music, before everything was stolen, on the banks of the Yonne.

The dispersive, unstable explosiveness of time.

Why are musical instruments so dark?

*

The mild, damp night, like the shadow inside a speechless mouth.

CHAPTER 26

Ovid's Pulsio

Ad veteres scopulos iterum divertor.

I allow myself to be dragged towards the old reefs.

The *veteres scopulos—veteres,* as in veteran.

I steer towards the waters where my boat has already capsized.

These are the last words written by Ovid at Tomis.

Ovid aged fifty-nine. Sick and dying.

So Ovid *diverts* himself with the *ancestral stones.*

These are the last words he addressed to Tuticanus.

*

The repetition compulsion is the force of the Erstwhile. The force that dismantles all obstacles, raises earth or bark or maternal skin, breaks dams, crosses frontiers.

*

Every day is the erratic Last Judgement.

Every age lets the Erstwhile stream through it—
the non-human, the tradition that is being forgotten
by the heirs, which lacks substance in the eyes of the
powers that be, which is omitted in repetitious inertia,
which is unconscious in fascinated humanity.

The enemy will go on constantly triumphing.
Death will go on increasing. What has to be transmit-
ted is the Lost Element.

*

For his writing paper, Manet designed a letterhead con-
sisting of a dark-blue scroll bearing the words TOUT
ARRIVE ['Anything can happen'⁴] in capital letters.

It was a device that took the form of a blue wave
rising above the paper and towering over what he
wrote.

This is the *pulsio* in person.

Everything happens and everything happens as
everything.

It happens as 'everything' (as world) and it passes
away as 'death'.

*

Our feet and hands were once fins. Our eyes are light-
hands. Blood is a liquid tissue. The myocardium—

heart tissue—possesses its own rhythmic pulse, its own spontaneous contraction. Its own temporal stimulus.

*

The two sources of time are connected. They become opposable only in the wake of language, by dint of the binary constitution of natural languages, dividing everything in the world by two, setting all things and speakers against one another in—polar, passionate, hostile, dialoguing, dialectical—pairs.

*

The Norse myths range two antagonistic regions against each other in the void: fog and sun, *niflheim* and *muspell*, death and warmth (*yang* and *yin*).

*

Fighting between animals fascinated the most ancient peoples of prehistory. It is possible that, before human beings, it fascinated animal groups themselves. Encounters between elks, the entanglement of antlers or horns—this matching of forces, this magnetization of potencies and oppositions, this strange binarization from before language, this pre-pairing struggle *represented* the selection of the males that dominated these groupings.

The fighting, selection and duels that still dominate them.

The troating of stags in November.

On the pre-human fight-to-the-death.

The bodily clinch of antagonistic forces (in reality, antagonistic *and* identical—mimicry to the death).

*

The social bodily clinch.

Homosexual competition.

The beauty of bookends.

The stranglehold, the collision.

The sexual embrace that is, so to speak, derived from symmetry, from mirror-image cellular division.

The flying buttress facing off against itself. Animal *fascinatio*—a single morphogenesis loses itself in itself, suddenly reformulates itself and falls to adoring itself almost to death.

*

When language seduces itself, it empties itself of its meaning in order to fascinate. It becomes primitive seduction, or, in other words, the ritual of addressing the other (and not seeking after truth or communicating a meaning). Language then becomes the abyss into which its own appeal falls.

Language then emerges as its own vertiginous attraction.

*

In the same way as celestial ellipsis and effusion form the same event, coming back and coming.

Re-passing precedes passing.

Seasonality preceded mortality.

*

The now—the *maintenant*—is the pre-eminent social delusion. But the *maintenant* maintains nothing. It is a co-presence of the erstwhile (the ageless lost element) and a threatening, extreme instability.

A binary conflict is constantly unleashing time. It is an endless, imageless jigsaw puzzle, but its pieces are living ones.

A game incapable of growing old. All the pieces are mobile. They are all active. All everlasting.

*

For the kitten playing on the lawn beside the river Yonne, time has no duration. The kitten seems *almost totally without memory.*

For the playing child who doesn't yet speak, time has the duration of lightning. It still has the animal status of ravening hunger. Tension, élan, *orexis*, the leap, the bound, eagerness. The intense, imminent, impatient *today*. At the extremes, it takes the form of the trance, of the journey of identification, of role-play.

*

In the trances of the first human beings there arose the problem of the loss of consciousness. This was the beginning of the vacillation in the sensation of being, since the problem posed with the trance is the problem of return.

The *puer* (from seven to fourteen), unlike the *infans* (from birth to seven), is return in person. He is recital by heart. Children are taught language and, with language, they are taught *returns*: the return from the square, the return from the sea-wall, the return from the beach, the return from holidays, the return home, the return of the year, the return of memories, language returning and going back again over its acquisition (consciousness).

Just as natural language is acquired, so too is the inexplicable return.

Paidagôgos in ancient Greek names the person who takes children to school and brings them home again. The Master of the Return Journey.

Language gradually permeates the body. Gradually return comes to fascinate the soul. Memory gets the better of desire and bounding infant curiosity disappears without trace, the way non-language evaporates into language. You believe that you can only miss what you have known. You dream that you can only desire what you have enjoyed. In hunger, as in knowledge, one wanders in the days of times past.

*

The earth, the world, the body, the brain—that is to say, the erstwhile, the past, the current, the unreal—never bring any halt to the one single passionate exchange between the period of excitation and the refractory period, between mastication and satiety, between delight and disgust, between reward and punishment, between desire and frustration, between rising and falling tide, between spring and autumn.

*

In the depths of time, an alternation between strength and weakness, incompletion and completion; between intense, accelerative proximity and a depressive, decelerative distance that is moribund and *largo* to the point almost of immobility.

*

Either dream or night, such is the *space* of the body, a real that is never real in the real until the moment of death.

Its extreme form of play.

That play in which an object falls and is then reeled back. The game actively produces an alternation between absent and present, hidden and seen, lost and found; this polarization between the invisible and the visible structures binary time. The first rhythm is that of disappearance followed by appearance. Nativity after life in darkness, the *nachträglich* followed by the first world—this is the primal pulse.

The strong beat—the downbeat—is loss. The upbeat is re-emergence. Reappearance is simply a repetition. The *pulsio* is merely a second time.

Only the strong beat—loss and birth—allow us to know the first time.

Language is retrodiction.

The first time occurs without experience. It is language-less.

On and off.

Alternation is the basis of time.

Departures and returns, obverses and reverses, *adrets* and *ubacs*.

Either death or life.

Ernst Halberstadt is the name of Sophie Freud's little boy who was playing with a cotton bobbin at his mother's feet while she was dying.

CHAPTER 27

Treatise on the Sky

It so happened that the Abbot of Marolles completed his *Lucretius* on the last day of October 1650.

On that day, as a preface to his translation, he wrote: 'But no one today deigns to lift his eyes to the sky and we weary of looking at it because it is so easy to see.'

There is no sky *in which the time is lost*.

To *read the time,* it is necessary to look at the sky.

Time is the sky.

When we lift our eyes towards the vault of the heavens, after the sun has faded at the furthest bounds of the earth, we are contemplating the *dark face of the past.*

CHAPTER 28

Primal Radiation

There is such a thing as primal radiation. Some nuclei date from 15 billion years ago. Their age is the age of the universe.

Potassium 40, thorium 232, uranium 238 have been giving off their invisible glow since the origins of time.

In the atmosphere, carbon 14 and tritium are constantly and imperceptibly giving off radiation and leaving their enigmatic traces in matter.

*

Walter Pater wrote of the small works left behind by the painter Watteau that they are lit by 'a certain light we should seek for in vain upon anything real'.[5]

Three centuries earlier, the Northern French, Flemish and Dutch painters cherished their colours.

They spoke of them with great regard and, indeed, with some fervour. They had the impression they were taking from the creator all the hues he had spread throughout the world at the time of its creation, which had taken him just a few days.

Van Eyck said that he painted with sunlight.

*

The universe no longer ends in the eighth sphere. What are now countless stars move through the silence of the night, not always twinkling.

The earth is a little more than 4 billion years old.

The moon is the same age, but has moved away from the earth.

The sun is older.

We revolve in a more or less stable orbit around a more or less stable star that is hot, luminous and perishable.

The solar system was born. It will die.

*

There is no time or space independent of the bodies that exist within it or measure up against it. The diameter of our galaxy is of the order of a hundred thousand light years.

Augustine wrote: 'Time is the being that lives in an inaccessible light (*lucem habitat inaccessibilem*).'

One day the oceans will boil.

*

The halting of radioactive exchanges enables us to date the death of biological individuals.

The radioactive half-life or 'period' of carbon 14 being 5,730 years, we use it to measure the traces left by human beings.

The radioactive period of potassium 40 being 1.3 billion years, we employ it to measure volcanic activity.

The radioactive period of thorium 232 being 14 billion years, we call on it to measure the age of the earth.

The period in which the intelligibility of natural languages remains active in the reading of books is infinite.

I contend that this is the measure of the lost element.

*

From high in the sky, 160 million years ago, raptors gave a face to the instinct to swoop and snatch away. Prior to predation itself, from the depths of the skies, nature quickens its pace nature quickens its pace in the elation that strives to invent aggression, rapidity and rapacity, before the apoptosis of death.

The milieu strives to spread into the bodies it invents for itself—the morphology of organs, spatial volume, the temporal dimension.

It evolves in the unknown and the unknown is itself.

It absorbs or, rather, ritualizes what it discovers about itself as soon as it is happy with it. What exceeds it may well be its end. Locomotion was the second face of time, a face tinier but more extraordinary than the explosion itself that is its Erstwhile, as it is the Erstwhile of space and the bodies it contains. Homochromes attract one another, just as homochrones respond to one another and are constantly sending one another the appropriate responses, the responses through which they fit together—like the betrothal songs which, in the past, locked certain little finches into monogamy.

In the order of time, homochrones are like reflections.

Synchrones are like the shadows cast by shapes struck by light, like the repercussions one sees in mirrors.

There are temporal chameleons that merge into the seasons and then into the ages like birds into air currents.

There are animals that are temporal ambush predators (angelsharks, night-hunters, lepidoptera dating back before man, mountain-dwelling birds of prey, readers of literature).

There is Erstwhile.

On the basis of this imprinting of forms in space, on the basis of this natural belonging, beings recognize what they do not know.

The knowledge they have mislaid staggers them.

A man who enters a Palaeolithic cave, even the first time he does so, recognizes it. He is coming back.

CHAPTER 29

Kant wrote that the senses do not produce time but suppose it (*supponitur a sensibus tempus*). Nor does succession engender it, though it does refer to it.

In the senses, time is ecstatic.

What the senses feel is the break-up of the There is.

Birth may serve as an image to time, provided that the Erstwhile is posited (it is posited in the *Urszene* that is inaccessible to any possibility of perception on the part of the person whose eyes will be the product of it).

Pais paizôn pesseuôn (child bearing-a-child playing-pushing).[6]

An expulsiveness in which the element of arrival always bursts forth more powerfully than what is happening or being lost).

The *infans* child is a primal radiation.

Ulysses is naked and drenched in water on the Phaeaceans' shore. His name goes before him. His story precedes him. Nausicaa plays the way Chronos plays. She pushes a rag ball. The realm of a child.

*

In the strange and very profound personal journal the emperor Marcus Aurelius wrote in Greek, the unity of the world, the earth, the sky, the remembering mind and the linguistic spirit that contemplates these things refer back to the homogeneity of the source. The *de natura* glair is the Roman seminal unity. A single drop of Erstwhile floods the universe.

There is this same certainty in the extraordinary *Metamorphoses* which proliferated from Ovid's pen with a violence bordering on the limits of natural power: there is no kingdom, race or genus; nowhere is there any impermeability of any kind. Only the sexual seeding of the world has unity.

Every life is at the end of time.

Every birth is from the founding of the world.

On the one hand: *in consummatione saeculorum*. On the other: *ab origine mundi*.

*

Everyone is searching for the origin: the depressive in his withdrawal; the city in its sacrifice; the drowsy child in the thumb he has pressed between his lips. The astrophysicist is searching for the origin of the universe and is constantly reinventing the scenario; the biologist goes after the beginnings of life, cultivating them within glass vessels; palaeontologists roam the earth looking for little bones with little bags.

The universe: 15 billion years.

Life: 4.5 billion.

Man: 100,000 years.

*

In my life, the bouts of antipathy-at-first-sight came at interstellar velocity.

Each time, I was stupefied to find myself hating so intensely people that I was just getting to know.

*

Above and beyond the force repeating itself in the depths of time, where does the de-synchronization attack come from?

One cannot even speak of an extension of complexity, so inconstant is this latter.

The terrestrial year lasts 365 days and its rotation period is 24 hours.

Mercury's year is 88 Earth days and its rotation period is 58 Earth days.

The Venusian year is 224 Earth days and its period is 243 Earth days, which means that on Venus the day is longer than the year.

Nature rushes in suddenly, jerkily, as a strange memory-form-information-recognition mass or ball.

The *Eurêka* of the propulsive Erstwhile which stretches—retroactively—into the space it invents.

When the attack becomes fascinated with itself, life invents death.

Where the past devours, at that point lies fascination. The derived form returns suddenly to the initial maw, to the protomorphic face where it swallows itself. Death is the *returning*, as expressed in the French word *regard*. A retrocession in a hurry, passing at great speed through all the temporal phases, decomposing into its tiniest elements, becoming once again disorganized life, then matter.

*

Seneca the Younger says it is Nature that gave the wild beasts, humans included, panoramic vision, in which she could contemplate herself in the quasi-celestial, envious, convergent rotation of their famished gazes.

*

Man cannot with certainty be described as the animal that forms the clearest view of his location when he observes it. ·

Certain flocks, circling in the sky, excel at this.

Their dance is finer than any walking or wandering.

*

At Rome in the 20s CE, Manilius wrote that it was sacrilegious to subject the heavens to language.

*

Some animals, in their silence and their belonging to their milieu, experience ecstasies that are perhaps onto-logically more powerful than ours, given our possession of language and our progressive, though intermittent, move away from nature.

Some autumn stags, shrouded in their mists, are more aware of the original thread of what is going on than the gods.

The sky suddenly absorbs the skylark into its blue substance.

With certain sparrows, imperceptibility devours them the way the vulture devours the hare;

or water the fish;

or Rome Caesar;

or the contents of a book the reader;

or the mother the child.

CHAPTER 30

The Snail

The snail appeared 650 million years ago with the coral on the ocean bed. Its shell is screw-shaped.

It moves by puckering up its body, roving around slowly on its shiny slime.

It moves like the ocean beneath the moon—by stretching.

*

A slime that isn't the track it leaves but the beginnings of the path it provides for its foot.

The snail loves only the dawn—or the sun that returns as the rain ends.

*

The moon agitates the seas. The moon stirs up the deep waters in the form of currents. The moon raises up their surface into rolls that break against the coasts, that die on the dressed blocks of stone, that hurl themselves against the currents of the rivers which pitch into the sea's waters.

In the hemisphere turned towards the moon, the oceanic masses stretch out towards that heavenly body as though there were an axis between the two planets.

The seas succumb to a remnant of the Erstwhile that still exerts its influence.

Time was when the moon was three times closer to the earth than it is today. The moon has detached itself from the sea like the mother who has weaned her child and is gradually, slowly, closing the bedroom door on his sleep.

Time was when the moon, adding its contribution to the sun more than four hundred times closer, played its part in raising the temperature of water during the night time.

CHAPTER 31

He died in 527 BCE at Pava in Bihar.[7] Yogindu said he was the last of the ferrymen who had renounced communal life with other human beings 'since the times of caves, springs and grottos'.

The precise meaning of Yogindu is the last moon. Literally, he is the last of those ferrying-to-the-other-side (the moon being typical of what ferries to the other side).

*

Yogindu said that already knowing is the opposite of finding out. We have to drive out the linguistic voice that embedded itself deep in the body in our obedient earliest days. The fire of mental concentration consumes what is repeated. There is no other way than the negative. Neither . . . nor . . . is the song proper to natural languages as soon as they are renounced. Inasmuch as it manages to free itself of language, meditation becomes once again a rebinding-the-world. Then the sun no longer stands over against the shadow that it casts but connects with a darkness from prior to its birth. The self connects with return. The pre-flowing source spreads a 'dull light' in the depths of every being. This dull light can be seen deep in the eyes of children, on the surface of the eyes of women as they climax and also, far off, in the furthest depths of the eyes of old people when they have lost all memory. It is a derived luminescence. It is 'light come from elsewhere' and this is the meaning of the word Yogindu. Parmenides also uses the expression 'light from elsewhere' to refer to the moon. But in the word Yogindu, lunar light does not mean that the light is the moon's.

Yogindu means the light that is not even light.

A dull luminosity that is born neither by repercussion, refraction nor distillation.

The light of no entity, which is found in nothing that is.

Light of pre-being.

Light that illuminates the beyond of the sun.

Light of lucidity.

The oldest self is joy at being reunited. This joy casts a glow with which all joy reconnects.

Yogindu wrote: 'Joy makes its abode in thought in an abrupt fashion, *like the migratory bird suddenly seeing the lake.*'

Yogindu wrote: 'The joy of the person contemplating what preceded him is exactly the same as *the joy of night* in the pure sky.'

CHAPTER 32

Piano

What has happened, say the shamans of Siberia, must be held in a semi-dreamlike state. If we wish to get the attention of the hunters who are listening, if we want what we are trying to say to register in their memories, we have to speak in hushed tones.

In Inuit, one of the many words for shaman is 'quiet mumbling'. This mumbling is half-way between the oral and the written. It is something like a regurgitation of spoken language that is already becoming detached from dialogue, is distant from the issuing of orders, and tones down the call element. A voice not unlike the little gulp of milk that resurfaces as a tiny white cloud on the lips of babies after they have been breastfed.

Against the background of this *murmur*—to use a Latin word—the rambling of old people, who have slowed their childhood babble, isn't in any sense to be scorned.

Thousands of peoples without writing bear witness to this; similarly, five millennia of writing-based civilizations establish this need for *mezzo voce* regurgitation as a hallucinated anticipation of a *de-oralized orality*.

They are seated in a ring, packed tight, small, their faces yellow, their eyes black as ink. Yet their eyes gleam and their faces seem to enjoy a mysterious inner lightsource. They gradually begin to listen to the soft voice, the sourceless voice, the hallucinogenic language, the hum that rises and returns.

*

What we call a shaman, the Inuit also call *angakoq*. *Anga* means the Old. To be very precise: the Before. The Old, the Before speaks in a peculiar way: he speaks with his eyes riveted on no object (this 'no object' is the ancestor of the book); the tone he assumes is deeper; he speaks hesitantly; he gives an impression he is translating, that he has seen something in the past, something very old, already shared, and difficult now to repeat. He half-swallows his breath; his voice withdraws half-way behind his lips and becomes a chewing in the back of his throat; the Before speaks in hushed tones.

*

This is also a music lesson—the absence of emphasis of dreams.

A lesson muttered once again, if possible, to the boards of the dividing wall. Or to the balustrade.

To the block of ice melting in the garden, as it drips away.

As it whispers.

*

The Before is the Predecessor in the same way as the animal precedes. The primal murmurs in the 'language before it acquires language'.

A pre-atmospheric immersion in sound—diffuse, obscure, maternal, focal, focalizing—an immersion that carries you along, that cradles you, that runs from left to right, that sings, that gathers together songs, origins, journeys and homecomings.

*

What day isn't born of yesterday?

In that case, where is the *hui*—the *hodie*, the today—of *aujourd'hui*?

*

Why has the word *piano* been sufficient in itself to refer to the *piano-forte*? Why, when it encountered narration, did human language shift to an undertone?

Why the book?

It is a curious thing that, for the volume of the body, mumbling in a subdued voice should be more calming than writing can be.

We see this with psychoanalysis in Vienna at Number 19, Berggasse: a couch, no face, a subdued voice.

I'm reminded of all that pre-digested prey reduced to a pulp that birds regurgitate into the beaks of their offspring to feed them.

We find a similar low mumbling in all societies when speakers of a language are alone for a long time. Through them the group speaks.

Confessionals situated away from prying eyes and places marked out for the baring of bodies in darkness weren't filled with resonant voices when the lost element was being regurgitated. When the lost element was being revisited, they didn't desire a harsher light. By reducing the range of the visible, black-and-white cinema nurtured narration through images in the same way as did the subdued-voice regime. In old films, it isn't particularly the direction, the acting or the plots I admire, but

I am dumbfounded by their stripped-down, highly simple vision, in which the contrast between black and white is the sole meaningful opposition. A vision that reduced the visible to its main difference, which is that between light and dark, from which sexual difference derived. It isn't dispersed into shadowless colours, the psychology of facial features, the stridency of voices, musical padding, the virtuosity of dance or the subtlety of shades.

Writers write in black and white.

There is no story that isn't a return.

Consequently, there is no piece of writing that doesn't necessarily bring back something from far off in what it is saying.

*

The calibration of an object (its value) is calculated by the number who have died for it.

The simple past is traded in the aorist on account of the numbers of dead that have punctuated the generations, that founded the families, that struck the alliances that were possible, that formed the groups.

The magic of the aorist in human societies is the wizardry of the incantation that is able to transmit the ancestral past (the primal force) into the fabric of present time.

The *basso continuo* of the world isn't the present.

Human beings are the favoured prey of the voracious monster of the emergent Erstwhile.

All human young are the fresh meat that falls to the Erstwhile.

*

The dramatic actuality of the past is everywhere at work in *the still-active entity*. Lightning. Predation. War. Typhoons. Volcanoes. The terrible 'acting-out' of Time in Being.

Flowers live only by the year—and that year returns.

In human beings—though they live only one life—there rises an age-old sap that goes back far beyond their own lives.

A voice that is *piano*, increasingly *piano*. *Pianissimo*.

*

Speaking forcefully diminishes one's force. If you shout, 'I love you,' you have already lost your sexual potency. You have to speak with your eyes. Between hunters, the intense, decisive exchange is a silent exchange of glances.

An *eye for an eye* before *a tooth for a tooth* is at the source of symbolization.

If predators spoke distinctly, the prey would be lost.

All cultural activities are infinite continuations of hunting.

*

Those who speak mysteriously of a thing they are talking about, circling all around it but not actually divulging it, clearly frustrate the people they are talking to of a meaning. But, by lowering their voices and indicating in roundabout terms—even by communicating their reticence—what they don't actually show, they transmit an old knowledge that has always been known: an old knowledge that will never be fathomed in our lifetimes.

In the same way that you can't really speak of the experience of death without dying, they are transmitting the meaning of a secret.

True secrecy belongs to what can never be shared; the Lost, separation, *sexus*, dreams, hunger, death.

The evocation that conceals evokes; that is what a dividing wall is.

Another life is sensed; or an unimaginable terror is defied.

Nightmares, dreams, ghosts regurgitate a kind of body on the dividing wall. That is to say, on the limit of our condition. That is to say, on the separated, sexed, grief-stricken boundary. Nightmares, dreams, ghosts cause the 'image' to hit an impassable wall—a wall one can only pass through in silence, with no possibility of return.

*

Antlers, horns, canines, claws, furs, odours, leaping, shrill cries, dull murmurings, where are you?

The megalithic societies became ancestor societies, societies with hallucinated dead voices.

Long-timescale, stone veterocracies towering, from the tops of the hills,

hills that were like skulls,

the settlements of wood and foliage of living human groups.

Societies with timescales as long as those of stone that calendared tasks while giving shelter to what spoke on behalf of longstanding traditions (hunting, returns, abstainings, feasts, solstices, festivals, births, grape harvests, sowings, marriages).

These intermediaries were initially the dead chiefs who spoke from beyond the grave, before turning into the ancestral tongues in which the gods would reveal themselves after enforced wanderings.

A stone-based timescale as lasting, insistent and circular as that of the sun's journey that oriented the alignment of the stones and, in orienting their alignment, oriented their shadows.

CHAPTER 33

The Solstitial Point

In the amphitheatre at Carthage where I was wandering with M, we suddenly came face to face with a deer that had its head turned to the rear and its front left leg raised. The deer was turning around in the act of grazing on the leaves of spring. This stag is one of the world's oldest represented themes. It is the solstice point.

The Latin word *solstitium* breaks down as follows: the sun (*sol*) suddenly stands still (*stare*) in its progress across the heavens, having reached its maximum boreal or astral declination.

This is 21 June or 21 December.

It is the longest day. It is the longest night.

Once it has arrived at this point, the sun-hero sets off on its way again, without turning back. We have here the prohibition on looking back. The sun, on its journey, inscribes the shorter temporalities of the seasons on the line it follows between these two points.

The coming and going between these two points invents the year as a first line of writing long before there is any written language.

*

Time knows no other direction than the one that wells up from the past. Reproduction is the source. Life is the accumulation of what it throws off, like an animal, into the stars.

Salmon go straight to the spawning ground to die.

All plants turn towards their erstwhile (the sun).

And, at the point when it returns, they flower.

Even the sun dances—makes an about-turn—on the day of the solstice.

*

Ulysses is Sinbad the Sailor. Where to go? He journeys to Ithaca. He goes back to his ancestors. He goes back to the original bed and the fig-tree wood that proves it. He gets back to the night where the scene decomposes and becomes invisible with each dawn. His father doesn't recognize him. His wife doesn't recognize him. His son doesn't recognize him.

Only his *hunting dog* recognizes him.

Only his *hunting wound* (the bite from a boar) identifies him to his wet-nurse.[8]

In ancient Greece, the elements of Being were, first and foremost, the Sun in the sky, the mountains towering over the earth, Chaos, Night and Hades.

Time was Typhon. The ancient Greeks sang magnificent anthems to Typhon: 'Thou who causest us to shudder, thou the irresistible, god of the unwarranted, immeasurable hours.

O hissing one, who moves about above the snows,

Being is the ancestor;

His acts are three in number: dawn, zenith, dusk.'

Rising, standing and lying down are the movements of the monster Being.

He devours the ephemeral ones in death.

There is a personal sun before there is a private *daimon*, a guardian angel (before an echo of internal language is born beneath the skull and resonates as the ceaseless, regular, identifying, domesticating murmur we call consciousness). We are put in mind of Philip of Macedonia's so very strange pronouncement in Livy: 'The *sun of my days* has not yet set.'

*

In ancestor worship, kinship shifts away from the verticality of the moment *hic et nunc*. It leans over to the horizontal, to the point where it becomes the boundary-line, the line tracing the threshold of the temple. It grows diachronic to the point where it becomes a chronicle set down in writing.

One day, the corpses of those who begat the young are no longer abandoned by them to the vultures and the wild beasts.

Parents are no longer devoured before the very eyes of their children.

The children hide them.

The prey that has been killed and humans that are deceased haunt the dreams of those who survive them to the point where they feel guilty.

The mix of hallucination and guilt occurs long before consciousness, which is something vocalized. But the two form the background to it.

The oldest human representations are images of looking back.

The muscle contracture that occurs in the necks of dying bisons is called *opisthotonos*.

They *seemed* to be turning around.

In fact they are dying.

Later, sacrifice plunged its knife into this solstitial fold in the neck, which arched around as though they were looking behind them.

With the antelope and ibex, the way they are looking backwards towards the pile of excrement coming out of their anuses—with a bird on top of that pile—implies that the spring is expelled by the dying winter.

And that the strong beat of temporality is driven on by death, which might be said to be its source.

By devouring vegetation and animals, the ogre Time lays waste to the earth, decimating all families and, indeed, all who live on it.

As the hunter hunts, as the world grows smaller, the belly of the temporal beast distends.

That belly suddenly explodes, gives birth, excretes. It brings forth the spring with new vegetation and animal young, repopulating the world with all that the beast of time had devoured. But I am over-interpreting little scenes scratched into bits of shoulder-blade. Always remember I am not saying anything certain. I am allowing the language I was born into to bring forth its oldest remnants which then mingle with things read and with dreams. The only thing certain is that a mythic plot is brought together here amid these incisions, these pigments, these stencilled hands, implying both a dream made of images and a narrative made of language.

*

Suddenly, the forests are in retreat. The ice is melting. The mountains rise up. We utter shrill cries.

Then come the Günz, Mindel, Riss and Würm glaciations.

Forests followed glaciers. Herds followed forests. Carrion hunters followed the carcases which fell from the herds that followed the forests which followed the glaciers that scooped out caves in the sides of the mountains.

What provides our sense of direction? Only the emptiness stretching out before us.

Voids and holes which we invade, as dreamers like to do in dreams.

*

We are still living in the interglacial period of the Pleistocene which we sometimes call present time.

Which brings us to Mallarmé's remark of February 1895: 'There is no present.

He who thinks himself his own contemporary is misinformed.'

CHAPTER 34

Curiously, I'd never looked back nostalgically on a world. I've never felt the desire to live in a past period. I can't cut myself adrift from our current potential resources, from the current possibilities for finding material in books, for shattered ideals, for the sedimentation of horror, for erudite cruelty, for research, for science, for lucidity, for clarity.

Having become so rare, never before has the sight of nature on the earth been so poignant.

Never before were the natural languages so revealed to themselves in their involuntary substance.

Never has the past been so extensive and the light deeper and more chilling. A mountain light or the light of the abyss. Never has the terrain been so dramatic.

CHAPTER 35

There are streams that meander about long before the human beings who follow them, the birds that fly above them, the flowers that border them. Secret traditions don't go back to historical periods. They re-emerge from the secrecy of the unmediated dispensation itself, beyond history, in the *fons temporis*.

CHAPTER 36

Mercury is a hard metal, dense and elusive.

Only the real is harder and has more holes in it; is more truncated, more sexed, cutting, dying.

Writing is closer to the real than speaking.

Writing is a denser material than mercury. I call up a face which each secret I divulge pushes further and further from me into the shadows, so true is it that all attempts to call out to people actually abandon them.

CHAPTER 37

After the Event

The past is constructed only after the event.

It is the second link in the chain that creates the concatenation with the first, thereby giving that first ring its particular nature, adding precedence to the spatial interval.

The dimension of the past opens up retrospectively without there actually being a present. In genealogical succession, where sexuality is concerned, the source is always *in absentia*. The present is what is being born, but never the conception. Our birthdays never celebrate our origins.

*

The exile of the ancient Hebrews who had been carried off to Babylon lasted from 587 to 538 BCE.

Judaism in the strict sense is post-exilic.

The relation between two times is time.

What comes after the event is time.

Just as the first man saw himself naked only after being sundered into pre- and post-lapsarian. Just as Hebrew was lost as early as the edict of 538 BCE (before returning as national language in 1948). Just as it happens that the failure of a return is seen in the return itself. Human time knows irreversible grief (mourning). In the retrospective knowledge of conception, human time experiences irreversible epiphany (birth). The post-coital does not coincide with the post-foetal which does not coincide with the post-natal which has nothing much to do with the post-Edenic. Such is the strange structure of time.

*

Writing decontextualizes language. To note down sounds with letters that fragment them wrests things away from the speaking that is entirely immersed in the cynegetic milieu and the balance of forces specific to the group. Writing brings into being a gap, a discrepancy. It disjoints dialogue which was previously indistinct and continuous. The letter is the staying, the deferring, the sabbatical, the—transitory or fallacious or mendacious or fantastical or fictitious—other world.

Writing institutes the *contre-temps*—the delay. Inventing the delay presupposes this prior possibility of temporality that language calls *temporization*. Man can take a step back in time as he can in space. He can negotiate 'time distances' (sequences, illusions, dramas, celebrations). He can furnish his compulsive impatience with instruments that count time; temporize to increase his pleasure by deferring it; register time to affirm its passing; build up expectation to intensify emotion; meditate; be ascetic or ecstatic.

Time can make the whole of temporality available.

*

Hadewijch says that above scripture, above all that is created, the short-circuit of the mind-that-loses-track-of-meaning recovers the lost element at the root of its loss.

Vision, then reading, then dazzlement,

Vision become reading.

Reading become dazzlement.

Vision, reading, then dazzlement recapture the irradiating intimacy of the wandering planets, letter for letter, atom for atom; they communicate at full speed;

without mediation, *sonder middel,*

they stream all at once.

CHAPTER 38

Praesentia

There came a day when I could no longer understand the present.

Why did a fragment of what spurted forth, wrested from that spurting itself, claim to be a reference point?

And I couldn't even think the present—*praesentia*—so much is it the case that thought itself—*noesis*—thinks nothing in the present. Thought is a part of the leaping and capturing. It is Erstwhile. It is what is lost. The lost hungry for the lost as the thing it lacks, which develops its appetite, 'procrastinates' its dream, extends its hallucination, delays its wait, freezes its 'leap' within its process of watching and 'lying in wait'.

We do not think by the second. The way time distends, it has the dimensions of a day about it, or a night, a week, a season, a pregnancy, a childhood; it takes the form of a ripening or decomposition, of regret, apoptosis, impatience, desire.

*

What is called the present is a phantasm found in all myths—it refers to the primal past as viviparous creatures understand it.

We see it in the clenched fists of the newborn, clinging to the memory of a furry pelt that hasn't been there for millennia.

*

The relation between the changed and the changing is continuous and lasting; it is always rhythmic, always binary: it abolishes the past slowly, devouring what occurs only in complete sentences, in whole rhythms; what dies or passes away it abandons in whole chapters, entire narratives, rather than in fragments or atoms.

*

Being and thinking are not the same. In the Greek of Parmenides, they are not *to auto*. In Cicero's translation, they are not *idem*. If we assume the real to be being, to be a-symbolia, to be an-iconia, then thinking is not the same.

Time as the alteration of the not *idem*.

Time is what unidentifies.

*

If perception were a genuine grasp of the present, and the present a dimension of time, then we could perceive neither succession nor speed.

There is so little difference between prediction and retrodiction.

Every linguistic narrative (genealogy, history, sociology, cosmology, geology, biology) consists in inferring from previous occurrences to summon up what is not currently here. The word 'presence' expresses this being-beside that is linked to pre-sexuality and is yet another instance of nostalgia for our uterine pre-home.

In Latin: *contrectatio*.

In English: *homing*.

*

The child being born is not synchronous with his origin.

Vestige and investigation are a single face. Whether we are speaking of the child in relation to his origins. Or the physicist in his confrontation with nature. Abandonment never abandons us.

I am speaking here of the unabandonable investigation of an infinite vestige.

*

The time of the apparition of the dead, the time of the hallucination prompted by hunger, the time of the phantasm of desire and the time of dreams represent the chronicle of the *ersatz*. In the time of the *ersatz* a past arrives and is immediately lost. It was there. 'I swear to you, *it was there*.' There is, founding the world, a There from before the time of being there.

*

The original has the dual dimension of the imminent and the past. The present is without presence.

Outopia.

Why can it not be?

Because it was.

The uterine place is that place-less place (that non-terrestrial pocket). And yet in the place-less place we all once lived. The scene our bodies presuppose is *outopia*; it has never been anywhere in the world that we have been able to see since we possessed sight. And yet we are the product of that scene and come from that world.

*

Sexus, tearing apart—the primal *abyss*. An operation in which all times and all places are rent in two. A head has to have two lips.

Heartrending lips, heartrending pages.

*

Time as *dimensio* is the second phase to time as *distentio*. Time becomes the continuous bond that makes it possible to unite events or objects which distension has disjoined or which language has first divided, then set against one another.

Time as binding agent corresponds to biological frustration in atmospheric life. It is acquired as a—more or less—calculable distance between need or desire and reward or enjoyment. *Capere* means to take. This is a much vaster *ceptio* or capture for that predator-imitating predator that is man. Per-ception draws from *dé-ception* (disappointment) what it aims for with the aid of anti-cipation. There is always a taking involved here—*une prise*: a hand that holds, that snatches, that grips, that retains. It is always about hand-holding, *main-tenance*.

*

What is the real?

How are we to 'name' the pole of the external world *that falls silent* as soon as language denominates it?

It is early January to the east of the standing stones at Carnac.

It is raining.

Before my eyes—insofar as I can see through the Brittany rain—I have the shabby remnants of plastic and iron that a river leaves when its level drops.

Time doesn't reside in the real (in the area left empty on the banks); it is the tide or the flood. The world's present isn't the original shore. The world is the site of the regretting of time (of the *regressus*—the retreat—of time).

The world may even be defined as a regretting of reality. A *nostos* of being.

The 'there' where language says that things aren't what they were isn't the old 'here'.

The scene in which nothing appears is the scene the epiphanic world doesn't contain. It is the scene that time doesn't count as synchronic. It is the scene that the air the body is as yet unaware of doesn't articulate in the form of bipolar signs.

CHAPTER 39

Aunque es de noche

Saint John of the Cross:

I know the wellspring that flows and runs.

From that hidden source both heaven and earth drink

though they do so by night.[9]

CHAPTER 40

Dreams

The first journey is being born. The dream of dawn is a journey. A journey from the womb to the light and back. A journey from the Erstwhile to now and back.

Then you raise your eyelids, you open your eyes.

*

During waking life, brain activity is often rapid, largely de-synchronized, entangled, linguistic.

Two phases alternate violently in the course of our lives, when we are unconscious in sleep. (1) During deep sleep, brain activity is copious, slow and synchronous. Breathing rhythms, heart rate and muscular activity gradually subside. These rhythms approach the limit of lethal deceleration. (2) During rapid eye movement sleep, the slow waves disappear. Brain activity becomes very lively and completely de-synchronized. The eyes, which are much more asynchronous than in the waking state, move in all directions and see whole series of images. The vulva distends and the penis becomes erect. Breathing grows more rapid.

Rest among humans is a state of quasi-lethal re-synchronization.

*

The tragic values inherent in the mind are the too-late and the after-the-event.

Contemptuous and fratricidal, we take little pleasure. We dream badly.

Read Job or Ptahhotep: the world at its dawn is old.

Blind Oedipus crawls around, goes astray.

Heroic values: we are primal like springs, eruptive like volcanoes, bloody like the newborn; we desire; we refight the Trojan War every century, every hour. From one hour to the next, everything is brand new. Every spring is more beautiful; every flower is the most disconcerting of the shoots of time, floating rapturously in the air, like the birds.

*

Feverish or anguishing inner excitation; quasi-sexual, wild de-synchronization; quasi-lethal, empty re-synchronization; empty skulls; images *in absentia*— all like organs of time.

*

The reconnection to the outer, atmospheric world has a counterpart in the slow-wave stage, the stage of profound disconnection, of quasi-coma, which comes close to the earlier inner night. Linguistic and communal oppositions, vital and sexual discords regress to a purely synchronic, low-frequency, high-amplitude oscillation that lies on the very fringes of Hell.

*

In the myths of the Australian Aborigines, entering a cave, dying, falling asleep and becoming-*phallos* all refer to a single operation.

Heroes are named the men-of-the-dream, the *phallos*-beings, the always-coming-forth or the *Imanka nakula* (the 'long time ago was'), as opposed to the *Ljata nama* (the 'now are').

The opposition is polar, but also chronological—the time of the Is draws sustenance from the time of the Was from which it comes. There is a world of silence and excitation before, and a world of the pulmonary drive and the penis, engorged or flaccid, after. In Being, the Were stand behind the Are, who still have something of the Were about them—to the point where they still dream of them. Because the Was has a meaning (an excitation) which is lacking in the Is, story cannot be distinguished from myth. The Australian 'once upon a time' takes the form 'Was-was'. This is the Dreamtime, the time of excitation, the time of the ever-erect totem. Every mythic plot ends with a man lying down and sleeping.

That is to say, with a hero who confronts violence and is admitted into a paradoxical state of youthfulness.

*

Canto V of *The Odyssey* opens as follows: On the shore of the island of the Phaeacians, Ulysses is naked. He is sleeping, exhausted after the shipwreck.

In Canto XIII, it is a *still-sleeping* Ulysses the Phaeacians send home.

Nausicaa, the banquet, the singing, etc., were just a dream.

Excited time has to be contrasted with ordinary time; hallucinating, desiring, lacking, hailing, singing, heart-rending time has to be contrasted with ease and with belonging to the environment. We have to contrast repetition in every sense and by whatever means with the inert state.

*

The dream evokes co-presence when that co-presence becomes impossible.

The dream presents. In presenting, it brings the absent to us.

*

Saint Paul wrote: 'The extremities of time are ranged against each other as *typos* and *antitypos*.'

In Latin, he would no doubt have written that, within memory, East and West stand opposed like *imago* and *sermo* [talk or discourse].

Between the involuntary image and the hallucinogenic voice stands the last kingdom.

Itself a restless tension between two poles that are always offset from each other.

Time as abyss.

One might call the tension, the gap, the relation, the opposition 'instant', and hypostatize that instance as an ontological dimension (the present). I shall do nothing of the sort. This relation to the two opposing poles is bigger than human history; it belongs to the explosion of the universe by which it bursts and pours into the void in the form of space. We cannot refer to the instance as a fixed point or a frame of reference that might remain stable, whichever way one looks at it. I leave the three dimensions of time to the philosophical myth-makers. Two dimensions of linguistic time are constantly in tension, in opposition. They are relentlessly rending things apart after the event. They are constantly throwing things out of synch, beginning from the dead interval. There is no peace.

*

To speak, to say *I* and to posit time are the same thing. To put it in Greek, *logophoria* entails *chronothesis* in the same way as consciousness is indiscernible from internalized linguistic vocalization. The agency that speaks, seizing hold of language in the *I*-function, refers to itself and marks the time of saying, when language returns in the two-term dialogue.

Strictly speaking, then, the *moment* is simply the assumption of the verbal function. Saying 'I' is over in a moment, but that moment is a long one—it takes a little more than 18 atmospheric months to arrive at this from the day breath first courses through our bodies.

The moment is long because it isn't immediate. There is non-synchrony. There is no coinciding here, but a lapse, a delay, the remnant of what was never originary. The endless remnant of the fall from Eden.

Every now—even now—has a content of 9 months + 18 months.

*

Only by burning does one carry the flame.

*

At the top of the cliff (Greek: *problēma*), overhanging the void (Greek: *abyssos*), the monumental Uffington White Horse.

CHAPTER 41

On the Uffington White Horse

Time is a galloping horse.

No man can stop it, since it is racing towards death.

Everyone sets out today to arrive yesterday.

The thing is to manage not to arrive.

CHAPTER 42

On Assuetude

Dependency is an irrepressible nostalgia for pleasures of old. An urgency on the body's part to return as quickly as possible to a state of excitation. To repeat the suddenness of much-loved joy, to recover the temporal effect of the thrill or *ersatz* or stroke of lightning that ran through the limb, body or skull. Flooding it with pleasure. There is a violently ecstatic pleasure that dominates the human and defines the attraction of oldest times.

*

Times of fable—the times in which storytellers set their tales—are always located half-way between absolute disorder and extreme opulence.

*

Times of fable are the primal scenes specific to history.

Civil wars.

Revolutions akin to cyclones.

Impenetrable forests.

Gardens of Eden on the eve of their fall.

Marches of time.

CHAPTER 43

The Countess of Flahaut

In the literary history of France, the Countess of Flahaut is *the* writer of nostalgia for the eighteenth century.

Writing as Baroness de Souza,[10] she waved her magic wand and transformed the terrifying eighteenth century into a golden age.

She turned the *ancien régime* into a paradise.

She was the grandmother of the Duc de Morny and the great-grandmother of Missy.[11] When Colette embraced Missy, she was hugging a part of her.

The first line of *Adèle de Sénange*, published in London in 1793, was: I have simply tried to show those things in life to which we pay no attention.

CHAPTER 44

The Handkerchief of Joy

At the end of the campaign of 1262, the Duke of Burgundy honoured the Chevalier de Vaudray before all the barons of his court, offering him command of his company of mounted crossbowmen, the most mobile of his troops. One winter, the company made an overnight stop in the town of Vergy. The crossbowmen all found billets for the night in the homes of the townspeople and farmers, without having to terrorize them with threats. The Chevalier de Vaudray and two of his men went up to the fortress to seek accommodation there. With her husband away, it was only reluctantly that the lady of the manor offered them the hospitality they were seeking. Given such a chilly reception, Vaudray was peevish in his thanks. Then the mistress of the castle and the chevalier cast their eyes on each other. Without it being their intention, they were astonished by what they saw and fell in love. While the chevalier's men were busying themselves in ensuring that dinner was prepared for them, the two yielded further to this visual curiosity which they could not control and which drove them towards each other. Nonetheless, when night fell, the chatelaine rejected Monsieur de Vaudray's attentions when he pressed himself upon her on the stairs. The chevalier's member was stiff and Madame de Vergy could feel it clearly beneath his clothing. He squeezed her thigh. But she said, 'My husband is away.'

The chevalier raised his hand. He gave his word of honour that he would not introduce any part of his body into hers. Still she rejected him. Then they stripped their loins naked in front of each other and pleasured each other with their fingers. A great spurt of liquid suddenly fell beneath the countess' feet.

The countess took one of her handkerchiefs. She wiped herself. Then she wiped her hands, Vaudray's hands and his member.

The chevalier discharged again into this handkerchief.

They fell asleep alongside each other. To be sure of his actions, as he slept, she kept Vaudray's member wrapped up in the handkerchief. At dawn he spilt his seed again. He left her. The handkerchief was stiff and had a wonderful smell to it. Madame de Vergy slipped *the handkerchief of joy* inside another one, on which she embroidered the letter V in pink thread, and placed it in the inside pocket of her gown. She died two months later from falling down stairs.

CHAPTER 45

Story of the Woman Called the Grey One

When Tafa'i became lord of Tahiti, he married a princess called Hina, which means the Grey One. She had long black flowing locks that reached right down to her feet. They came to know each other and to love each other. When Tafa'i left, she died.

Tafa'i came back from his travels. On the shore he learnt that Hina was dead. He resolved to go immediately to the land of the dead to join her. He slit his throat. He went to Tataa, some 20 miles from 'Uporu, the place where souls meet up before departing for paradise. At Pa'ea he learnt that his wife was already on Mount Rotui. He rushed there, climbed to the summit, but again found she had already left. Undaunted, he got back into his canoe, reached Ra'iatera, climbed Mount Te-mehani and came to the spot where the two paths diverge. Tafa'i spoke to Tu-ta, guardian of the entrance to the paths. Had Hina been past this spot? To his great relief, Tu-ta replied that she had not. As Tu-ta saw it, she must be hiding in the bushes and getting her strength back before flying off, launching herself from the top of the cliff.

So Tafa'i hid. He too gathered himself and waited. Hardly had his breathing eased when he heard the sound of leaves being disturbed. He realized that a god was speaking to him. So he crouched down, his eyes wide open, ready to spring. Presently he saw before him the tall, wondrous figure of his wife. She was dashing towards the rock. But before she could take flight from the Stone of Life, Tafa'i made a prodigious leap into the air and caught her by the hair. She had an enormous mane of hair and, by plunging his fists into it, he managed to pull her back. She struggled but her husband held her firmly, dragging her back to the Stone of Life. While this was going on, Tu-ta had run up and was explaining to Hina that the time had not come for her to leave this world and that she should, rather, turn around. Then she turned around and saw who was restraining her by her hair.

'It's you, Tafa'i!' she said.

Then she rested her head on her husband's neck and closed her eyes. She was purring. They went off into the bush and lived again. Since they were living on the margins of this world, they were far removed from any social or family life. They were both filled with joy. They were in love. They held each other's hands and wandered along the cliff tops on the edge of the abyss.

CHAPTER 46

There are men who follow the banks of rivers with the aim of getting back to their source. They climb mountains. They come up against solitary wild beasts. They discover wondrous women. They think of themselves as the companions of the great silent birds of prey flying at great heights—on top of the world—sweeping up the moon and sun in their talons, and swooping down suddenly amid the steep rocks and fearsome flowers to crush their prey and drench them in their blood. They keep watch over some harrowing spots. They live for a time in caves inaccessible to ibex and bears. They fear neither sky nor night.

Most let the breezes carry them along and dive into the sea before suddenly turning around as the sun does twice a year.

Some men go against the flow.

There are centrifugal men, men who go against the flow, just as there are rivers that flow into others. From the beginnings of time, there are anti-focal, anti-festive, anti-social men. Mountain men. Stag men. Fountain-head men.

CHAPTER 47

Nietzsche was a salmon man—attributing earlier dates to things, regressing, returning, returning eternally, as the stars continue eternally to desire.

The Pacific salmon travels up to 2,000 miles to spawn and die. A *regressus* of 2,000 miles.

A counter-gift, a nostalgia that is pre-human, keeps time moving.

Because a gift, a present which is the past—that is the way the round-dance goes.

The magical trance is an extreme round-dance. Music removes time from language, and detaches *what comes* from the linearity out of which it proceeds and the death that interrupts it. The round invents the past that stands before you. Music is what makes the past go round to the point where it returns.

Spinning top, wheel, *iunx*, rhombus, spool, spindle, spinning-wheel—all of them rotations that emit a sound, that hum as they spin.

The gyration of the earth.

The dizzying whirl of trances.

*

Captain Hatteras was afflicted with polar madness, as is the dawn.[12]

As are salmon.

As are the moving stars of the zodiac.

Walking straight ahead, then changing direction and walking backwards along the path of Sten Cottage Asylum, Captain Hatteras is as one with the rite of passage that is the trek to the North.

*

When sorrow becomes unbearable to the skull, even men lose their coarseness. A sense of decency forms on their lips and they fall silent.

CHAPTER 48

On the Happy Ending

Even before he can conceive of such a thing, the two-way arrow haunts the hunter's mind. It is so difficult to make an arrow. It is so difficult to find one's way back again.

In ancient China, the myths are full of corded arrows.

In Australia and North Africa, the two separate inventions of the boomerang occurred—that weapon which returns to the hunter's feet the way his dog does.

In the Palaeolithic caves, the bison with the bulging neck and the fawn looking back over its shoulder are there to encourage the return of the sun.

Going hunting, killing, returning and recounting the hunt to your hearth-group when you bring back your prey.

The schema is threefold at its source, since killing, returning and telling are the same thing. To tell is to have conquered, to survive and to be back. It is to return from the hunt with the dead game as the third element, as proof, and with the story to narrate into the bargain.

The problem for shamans doesn't lie in travelling a very great distance, an infinite distance (drugs, the death-defying trance). The problem that faces them is the problem of their return. An auxiliary is needed, a reference point, an *inoa*, a bird-stick.

The hunter, like the shaman—these are the first two human social specializations—needs an assistant-in-retracing-his-steps.

*

The last part of the last sequence of a myth is necessarily positive. There are no exceptions to this rule. Every story presupposes a survivor. The notion of the happy ending is founded on this. That foundation is tragic. You have to have returned from the ordeal to be able to recount it to everyone. If the prey has devoured the predator, if the shaman has become lost in his ecstasy or bodily spasm, if the species has been wiped out, if the nation has been exterminated, then there is no story because there is no one to tell it.

You can't even say the story ends badly for the victims—it isn't even told.

The end of the narrative is the telling of what has been undergone (it is the same with hunting, the same with the shaman's trance, the same with psychoanalysis).

What stands opposed to being-able-to-come-back-and-tell? Death (or madness in the case of trances).

It isn't the achieving of the great feat, victory in battle or the solving of the problem that constitutes the end of the hunt, the competition or the war. The end is returning-to-tell-the-tale.

*

One cannot distinguish between beauty and an abyss of sadness.

*

Three times or tenses hang together: the ordeal, the semicircle of return, the telling within the group that constructs what was undergone in the ordeal.

This is why the tense of the telling is *always the past*. (It's never the time of the ordeal that prevails in the telling but the time of telling-what-was-undergone-without-the-group after returning to the group).

Corollary I: Why does every narrative begin with a calamity? Because every narrative reports the story of a death, either animal or human.

Corollary II: Why does every narrative finish on a happy ending? Every story ends in a kind of elation because the joy of having killed, the joy of still living and the joy of telling are indistinguishable.

CHAPTER 49

On Palaeolithic Guilt

The foetus eats its mother.

The hunter eats the wild beast.

Palaeolithic guilt is an obscure sense of having done wrong that is attached to eating something stronger than oneself and more alive than oneself.

With your hands still stained with the blood of the hunt, you fear the vengeance of the prey that has been killed.

You eat that prey and a re-morse glimmers for each morsel you take from the body that is other.

Detrivorousness, carnivorousness, cannibalism— man eats what is past.

Man steals past from the Erstwhile.

*

The phrase 'In the past men were still animals' means: 'Before natural languages, beasts were not yet the opposite of men.' Beasts were not beasts. In the past, men and beasts were not distinct. There was no cooking, no trade, no marriage, no funeral rites. Only reading existed as yet, and the practice of reading dominated the world. All forms of excrement spoke. They were the spoor that identified every absent being to every present one by smell and by sight as creatures roamed around.

*

There are constantly two beats pulsing within the 'before' of time. At the heart of the *adventus* [the having-come] of the Coming and within the Advent itself. Prehistory before history. The mother's heart before our own.

Two silent lives precede accession to language. The temporal structure is constantly being battered and displaced by the ahistorical thrust. Cultural instability is constantly being torn apart by the animality of the source-species. A dangerous boundary line is constantly shifting, a front line where war is endless, where all that is buried explodes, where all that you eat roars, where every thwarted muscle movement or sensory impatience protests.

The always-lost-of-what-we-were-in-order-to-become-what-we-are lingers in us as the unknowable or obsesses us as the rejected. The constantly unknown that is concealed by identity or roles or illusion or consciousness is the blind spot of vision—or, rather, from before vision—of predation, then of the narrative, zoological and, subsequently, human quest. We pursue the anxious, ever-hungry activity that haunts our destinies. Sometimes, in the best of cases, that worried, impulsive avidity cuts into our lives and devastates our days. At bottom, the soul is neither binary, identical, negative, judicious, directional, narrative, progressive nor symbolic. In the beginning, everything revolves—like the sky, the stars, matter, life, nature, sexuality, the seasons. Even the true self is a false self. Become what you are—but there isn't anything that has to *become*. We are in no way the sort of thing language refers to. We are, at best, *in-formis*, hunger, *meta-morphosis*, a question, *curiositas*, audacity, tension, a springing, a leaving, a coming-out-of.

*

Marcus Aurelius wrote that the light of the sun is a single entity, even though walls, branches of trees and the sides of mountains divide it up. The substance divided by dreams, hallucinations, proper names and human languages is also a single thing.

*

Language transformed differences by setting them against each other term by term, in keeping with its systematic, aggressive, dual, binary madness.

Vitality was set against order, woman against man, mother against child, red against white, blood against sperm, flesh against bone, birth against death, womb against tomb.

Scholia. Language based on oppositions no longer differentiates. Setting everything against everything else, it binarizes everything. Uncoupling everything, it symbolizes everything. Symbolizing everything, it breeds conflict.

Through language we cease to be two-phase creatures, creatures of two sexes and two worlds, and become beings in whom two phases of time are opposed, in whom two sexes envy each other and two worlds collide.

We fall prey to conflicts which themselves have two phases, in which two sexes stand over against each other in twice two relations of kinship—conflicts that are unceasingly anachronistic, but a hostility that is chronic and unquenchable.

CHAPTER 50

Urvashi

The nymph Urvashi, standing motionless in the night, told King Pururavas: 'Beat me three times a day with your stick, but, whatever you do, do not show yourself naked!'

Alas, after four seasons had passed, a storm that blew up as night was drawing to an end caused her to see him naked. Her husband was illuminated by a flash of lightning. The lightning went on until day dawned from it. At that point she disappeared. At least King Pururavas thought she had fled.

He set off to look for her.

He wandered for years.

One day he came to the shore of a lake that was thick with swans. He gazed on them, then observed them closely. He recognized one as his wife.

The king approached this swan, saying: 'Why did you abandon me?'

Urvashi said: 'I didn't abandon you. I saw you naked. I became dawn and flew off by my own light.'

Pururavas said: 'If you don't come back to me, I shall hang myself from this willow tree.'

She said: 'Don't do anything of the sort. Spend the last night of the year with me, but above all sink yourself deep into me!'

King Pururavas returned from that night with a little child, holding it by the hand. From that day onward, fire became mimosa.[13]

CHAPTER 51

Motionless as night was falling, I watched the white house with the six green shutters. I saw a light go on in the upstairs rooms. Two downstairs windows were lit.

I saw the white Simca in the moonlight.

CHAPTER 52

You can close books, leave women, change cities, quit jobs, climb mountains, cross oceans, pass borders and board planes all you like, but your dream always stays with you.

CHAPTER 53

On 'Backwards'

In trances, the body *falls over backwards*. Every image of the human body swaying with upraised arms and preparing to fall to the ground on its back represents the moment of trance—a time of *petite mort* when speech rambles and you don't know if you'll come back alive.

The passage to the other world is a way of saying the passage to the world *in illo tempore*.

Not a world *ab origine* but the first kingdom of the pure Erstwhile.

The pure Erstwhile is the pre-worldly world in which predators and prey had not yet broken off their savage polarization.

They still spoke the same language (cries).

Animal 'calls' are instruments that imitate the particular cry of each animal to bring it to them.

We give the name 'decoy' to wild animals, caught alive, that are tied up and starved and, by crying out, attract wild animals of the same species.

At its dawning, music was distress-calling-the-fellow-creature.

Roland sounds his horn.

Dido hails Aeneas.

When did the mere fact of calling bring someone to us?

In childhood.

In our—indiscriminately animal or human—childhood. Childhood when it is happy. How are we to define happy childhood? *The cry brings the mother.*

The strident tears of the infant summon the breast that slips between the lips that suck from it.

To write is still to call, in the sense that pure-silent-calling brings pure-lost-motherliness.

*

Time doesn't exist but the past exists—it comes from sexual reproduction which determines the succession of generations by their disappearance into death. Ancestors precede the past.

*

Olden times in ancient societies are defined as dream time. In dream time, *killed animals return*, their killing returns, as do the sharing-out of their flesh and the manducation to which their sacrifice leads. The feasts of yore, long-dead hunters and the memories of their hunts return.

Olden times divide into the recent and the erstwhile. The past gathers everything that happened in bygone days into the experience of the dreamer.

Nature is olden times as the Erstwhile (genesis, animals, being, the wild).

A distinction can also be made between the pre-diluvian (the glacial periods) and the post-diluvian— the rise of water levels when the climate suddenly heated up in 12,700 BCE.

*

At Sumer, the god Anzu, the lion-headed storm-bird, steals the tablet of destiny from the god Enlil. The hero Ninurta tries to kill the god Anzu with his bow, in order to take back the tablet from him.

But the reed arrow doesn't strike the body of the god Anzu.

The arrow comes back.

The god Anzu has told the arrow that was heading towards him: 'Reed that comes towards me, go back to your reed-bed. Imagined form of the bow, go back to your forest. Bowstring, go back to the sheep's gut. Arrow-feathers, go back to the birds.'

The magic practised by Sumerian scholars consisted in sending all cultural artefacts back to their original elements.

In the same way as the shaman-healer sent evils back to their worlds.

In this same way the gods can dissolve into pre-birth those beings that have been born.

This is what death is for the ancient Sumerians—the return to the elements. The molecule decomposes again into its atomic Erstwhile.

Etymology is the art that enables literary people (specialists in letters) to dissolve entities into their elements.

*

By the tomb of Semele at Thebes, an illegitimate son cries out at his mother being incinerated by Zeus' lightning.

The forest cries out at the town—at its granaries, spears, temples and ships.

Beasts cry out at the animal which drove them from life by consuming them, which drove them from their dominance by stealing their cunning, their skins, furs, feathers, teeth and antlers, which, through the use of speech, drove them all from the Garden, which tamed a large fraction of them and penned them up in the first townships.

Nature cries out to have its land restored to it by humanity.

*

In the early years of the twentieth century, Sir John Marshall excavated the cities of Mohenjo-daro and Harappa. He dug up a host of seals bearing scenes of people looking back. The script he exhumed made use of 400 symbols that are still undeciphered.

In the last years of the twentieth century, Jean Clottes, pushing open his car door and showing me the enormous, dark mouth of the cave of Mas-d'Azil, held out his hand and exclaimed, 'The rubble of the last century!'

This is what the prehistorian meant: the finds, which were indeed Palaeolithic, had been scattered downstream when the road was built at the end of last century.

The carvings on the bones were lost for ever, perhaps without even having been glimpsed by the roadbuilders who destroyed them.

There and then at the Mas-d'Azil, beneath the vault above the river, I jotted down this expression that is so remarkable inasmuch as we incline to signify identity in the destruction of the source itself that is within us.

All human beings are 'the rubble of the last century'.

CHAPTER 54

Animals

Far away in space and time, the context for fiction, being necessarily a questioning about origins, is situated in the other place, the other time, the place beyond the frontier, the *saltus* beyond the *limes*, in far-off reaches, in wild lands, in the violent, unpredictable, never-known, always timeless past.

The unknown cleaves to the unknown, from which one can gather strange rituals that form the substance of the tale one brings back with them.

Mezzotints, a woad cart, *azulejos* panels, the seventh string—these are the things I can be said to have brought back from the other world.

Being something primal, the background is always maternal (the mistress of the animals, nature, violence, night). The hero is always a possible son-in-law.

Three recurrent time-schemes converge in every human story: (1) rebirth as change of season (the son-in-law kills the father-in-law, the young man kills the old one, a Frazerian royal succession); (2) rebirth as second birth (the son-in-law is initiated in the forest in three perilous ordeals, initiation at puberty); (3) rebirth as victory over death (the hero, after a long journey to the land of the dead, comes back among the living, *nekkhuia*).

*

Even Christianity didn't disrupt the lineaments of folk tales. This is an Erstwhile that can never age; an Erstwhile that is Youth par excellence beneath the maternal gaze (the young future son-in-law, the future husband-to-be, the avenging son after fraud or injury, the knight with gauntlet or lance). The morphological inertia of the three-phase narrative precedes the story it shapes. All tales, from whatever age they come, refer to an absent springtime, to a mythic matrilineal society and to a Palaeolithic world in which humans and animals form the basic pairing, each group dividing into the solitary and the gregarious.

*

In the most ancient myths, looking back is forbidden on pain of the death of the one looked back upon. At the solstice the sun must not look back. You aren't going to go back in death's direction. You aren't going to regress to the preceding winter. You have to press on again, head down, towards the springtime.

We see this in the wondrous, delicate head of the fawn at Mas-d'Azil.

Rückblick.

The idea running through Müller's work also ran through Schubert's—the idea of happiness belongs to the looking back, the obsession to past love yielding gradually and imperceptibly to love of the past.

Wilhlem Müller died at Dessau on 30 September 1827. I loved Fräulein Cäcilia Müller. Müller knew nothing of Schubert setting his *Winterreise* to music.

*

Müller: 'Where is green grass to be found?

In the world of memories.

If my heart is blood that flows

all that flows is my face.'

The whole of the *Winterreise* is merely a dream of spring.

Time suddenly thaws. Then nature is all streaming joy. Springs and mountains are thawed time. The melting of the past is time. The streaming of the Erstwhile is the spring.

*

Unhappiness is distinct from despair.

Unhappiness consists in the belief in the present. The unhappy body is the body that excludes the possibility of any past affecting it. Depression, *acedia* have a panic fear of the past welling up again here like a devouring wild beast. The depressive aspires to live in the moment. All memory must be avoided. It carries too much emotion. All looking back is avoided.

The mark of dereliction is the inability to suffer the past, because *the possibility of happiness forms a powerful bond with the Erstwhile.*

*

What is the invention of psychoanalysis at the end of the Austrian empire? A *passion*, consumed in the form of language, *for the passing of the past.*

*

The passion for the past has such power over the mind that the Jews, when wandering aimlessly in the desert, couldn't appreciate the bread of the angels as it fell from the sky.

They snubbed that manna, even though it had the miraculous power to adapt itself to everyone's taste.

They pined for the food they had eaten in Egypt when they were slaves.

*

For the Akkadians, the future was situated behind human beings. What was before their eyes was the past. What lies behind men's backs are the future problems that are going to come upon them like a wave, a wild beast, some flood or upsurge. Making an about-turn means putting everything you have experienced behind you: parents, masters, sources of terror, etc.

*

Playing on the Greek word *meta-odos* (after-path), Marcel Granet said that all who spoke of method were engaged in mere retrospective *waffle*.

The method is the path after you have travelled it.

The path-after is the return-path.

We should add: The return path is the outward path becoming trace *by being lateralized on the left*.

*

Animals too, at least all the vivipara, have this initial lost world deep inside themselves, this world whose empty trace affects them. It drags them into melancholia. It comes back in their dreams. They renounce it in their enormous sighs.

*

In the prehistoric caves, the beasts whose outlines are painted on the walls aren't the ones that were there. They aren't the everyday ones (reindeer, dogs). In the mystery of the Eucharist among Christians, it isn't bread that's there in the bread; in the wine that's there it isn't wine. It's human flesh and blood that haunt them. The lost element endlessly brings back violent predation with it—imitated, guilty, unpardonable predation, the old primal hunt. Everywhere we find dead wild beasts being consumed by groups of people.

CHAPTER 55

On Force

On Semele, Zeus' thunderbolt victim.

Semele is the mother of Dionysos the Wild. Dionysos is the Untameable, the Erstwhile, the Master of Wine who is himself the son of Lightning.

All psychotropic substances attract one another mutually.

All 'highs' cluster together under the sign of the lightning flash.

*

In Latin, *vis*, *virtus* and *violentia* are the same. In *vis*, force and gushing-forth are mingled. *Vis est pulsio*. Excrements and stains have a marvellous generative power, gushing forth like the life to which they attest. Children, faecal matter, urine, vomit, sperm and tears all gush out of the body like births.

*

In *vis*, laughter and force are connected—laughter is opening. An opening that opens the openings.

Humans *piss themselves laughing*.

Laughter brings out of the cavern of the body a kind of sunshine or force that bursts out.

Bringing the sun out of its cavern in Siberian myths, in American myths. Bringing the bear called spring out of its European cavern where it hibernates, where it spends the winter in its ossuary, surrounded by its scratchings on the walls.

*

Izanagi lay with Izanami and their congress gave birth to the islands of Japan.

Then Izanagi lay with Izanami and their congress gave birth to Amaterasu, the Sun.

Then Izanagi lay with Izanami and their congress gave birth to Kagutsuchi, Fire. Now, Fire burnt the vulva of his mother as he passed her lips and Izanami died bringing Kagutsuchi into the world. Incensed with sorrow, Izanagi killed his son Kagutsuchi and descended to the realm of the shades to look for Izanami. But, returning from the Underworld, Izanagi turned around and was gripped with terror at the spectacle of death on the face of Izanami.

He abandoned his wife there and then. He fled. And he blocked the entrance to the Underworld so that his wife could not come and join him in the last kingdom.

Amaterasu, the Sun, daughter of Izanami and Izanagi and the elder sister of Fire, took refuge in a cave.

So the earth no longer had light.

All the *kami*—the spirits—of the skies gathered before the entrance to the cave to which the sun had fled, in an effort to bring her out. They danced before the entrance.

They danced for years but the sun didn't come out.

One day, Ame-no-Uzume exposed her private parts as she danced. Everyone laughed. Amaterasu wanted to see what was causing this wild laughter. She came outside, saw the obscene dance of Ame-no-Uzume with her exposed vulva and laughed and the beaming light of her laughter lit up the world.

*

Ame-no-Uzume is Baubo.

Vis merely conceals sexual *violentia*.

Angry violence and the release of laughter alternate rhythmically. They punctuate the universe: erstwhile and genealogy, source and woman, volcano and cave.

Colère—anger—is the old name for coition and recalls the massive monstrous hunger of winter in which a mortally wounded *alter* prowls.

Laughter is a continuing expression of the unstaunchable haemorrhage of birth. It is the bison-headed woman on the end of the stalactite in the Chauvet caves.

A haemorrhage we see also in the well scene in the Lascaux cave at Montignac.

A wounded bison, with its belly open and haemorrhaging—solar creature, turning its head around.

The turgescence of the hunter. An upsurging in the night of the cave in the same way as erections are the hallmark of dreams. An upsurging of the first sign in the first man killed. The Sacrificed One. The Dead One. The God. The Crucified One.

Marcus Aurelius wrote: 'The sunlight spreads everywhere but never runs out.'

Parturition, bloody explosion, dawn, fever, haemorrhage, outpouring, bursting is the oldest figure of time.

Waters before the waters.

The old deluge from before there was dry land or forests and rivers.

CHAPTER 56

The Unthinkable Coming Through

At the end of ancient Greek tragedies, the leader of the chorus repeats the ritual formula: 'For the unexpected the gods find a way.'

The formula implies that there is a way through (*poros*) for the unthinkable (*adokéton*).

Such is the nature of the time contemplated by the citizen-spectators who have come to sit in a semicircle in these first days of spring, before sacrificing the Goat of Seasonal Change.

Where the *aporia* is concerned, there is a way through.

The gods bring to pass the events that men do not foresee. Time is not within the sphere of men but of a surging-forth.

A disconcerting gushing-forth.

The unthinkable coming through.

Human societies are not always able to ensure the return of the expected. The gods are even more polymorphous than the seasons. The future is unknown. Only the gods in their bottomless depths (their abyss), in their limitlessness (their aorist), in their unseeableness (Hades) can put an end to the sudden.

*

They say that in simiomorphic societies tombs are found before the *sapiens sapiens* stage.

How an ancestor was made.

Neanderthals, like *Homo sapiens sapiens*, buried their dead.

They invented a *beyond* running alongside the biological environment. That beyond is attested to by burials, then stones, then *agalma* and funeral rites. They established festivals to impose happiness (or at least absence of resentment) on that other place where all the ancestors of the living come, one after the other, to reside.

Paradoxically, but inevitably, by inventing that beyond, they gave birth to a place before the lives of the living—an Erstwhile from which they derive their faces, their names, their language, their colours, their clothing, their ways.

Among human beings, death consists in transforming the deceased into ancestors. In turning corpses into inhabitants of another world. In pinning those able to return in dreams to a place they cannot easily get out of—or one they neither need nor wish to leave. In transforming the Lost into an Origin.

Society recycles the social identity whose fleshly underpinning fades. Features, forenames and personal foibles go round in a loop. Society doesn't die. Protecting oneself afterwards and rooting oneself beforehand are the same.

Shut out as corpse, the deceased is produced as ancestor by gifts and the symbolizing offering of the newborn. In this sense, the ancestor is the opposite of the corpse. Through death rituals, human beings transform the After into Before and the Before into Advent.

*

The past is an immense body and the present is its right eye. But its left eye?

What does the left eye see?

With Sardinian and Corsican stones, an open eye and a closed one—and, in their shapes, the *vulva* and the *fascinus*—alternate on the same polished stone.

The universe works by twos, which is the same as repetition. The kernel of astral, material, vital functioning is repetitive. *Encore* is its secret.

*

Human heads are neither one nor three. Every coin has its reverse or its obverse. Every mountain has two sides.

*

The Hittite annals entitled *The Tale of Zalpa* begin with the abandonment of thirty daughters, set adrift in baskets on a river.

The gods rescue them.

They go to Tamarmara to thank the gods.

But on the way, at Nesha, the thirty sons fail to recognize these thirty women as their sisters and, on the orders of their mother who doesn't recognize any of them either, mate with them. They beget the months, the days and the nights.

*

In the Louvre, a remnant from the palace of Sargon is on display. It is a large black stone on which King Sargon is sculpted in relief, offering an ibex and a lotus flower as gifts.

There are two ways that the milieu into which we surge forth is appropriated. The Erstwhile is either hunted or gathered. Both the hunted and the gathered, each having been wrested from Nature, are sacrificed, so that she will renew them annually. This sacrifice forces Nature into the more generous counter-gift. This is the regal function: gamekeeper and gardener (zoophile and phanerogam).

In ancient India, cut flowers served as substitutes for game animals when it hadn't been possible to find any on a royal hunt (when the Erstwhile had been too wild to allow itself to be caught).

The flowers on their branches are no more seasonal than the young of the wild beasts. The clock they represent for us is merely more regular and less changeable.

*

With humanity, life did not recoil before nature, the environment, meteorology and the stars, but it gave in to what is lost, to frenzies, dreams, phantasms, reflections, symmetries, ghosts, words—to all the hallucinations of thought.

That is why, with humanity and its harrowing, prattling neurosis, the future came more and more steadily to assume the appearance of the past.

*

A drugged species rushes towards the strongest part of what it has experienced. Towards the most violent, bloody, hallucinatory element of what stirred it into being.

*

Issa said of the spring: 'The snail twists its body to look at its trail.'

*

A circle of 300 broken stalagmites and stalactites dates from 47,000 BCE.

Animals biting their own tails.

Bringing back what was beforehand—the strong beat, the *primum tempus*, the sap, the shoots, the young, migrants, birds, flowers, the son, salmon, wild beasts.

*

The feeling of coming back to somewhere, of recognition, of obviousness, the sense of being 'hot', the sense of familiarity, inexplicable assurance, the oceanic feeling, the impression of déjà vu, of having lived through something before, of having known it beforehand—all these little spontaneous trances that invade the body with such exhilaration take you, at the same time, to an area verging on anxiety. A *limes* where omnipotence confronts anxiety. We are right to fear not being in control of what is happening; we are mad to believe that we ever are; we wander between time's two poles. We are like the kites or yo-yos children keep in the air between sky and earth, between *endo* and *exo*, between sea and land.

Like the sea's undertow.

We can never be sure of coming back. But what comes back within us in these impressions isn't anything that can entirely disconcert us, because it happened. It is the pure past launching its wave. It is the Erstwhile. The past before memory. The oceanic, aoristic, aporetic, abyssal, limitless plenitude from before we were separated, before the object was lost, before we became sexed and developed breathing.

*

The maximum of unpredictability we can hope for from the future is an active reverberation of the past. A de-retro-activation of action. Not anticipation (which is the past leaping into a repetition programmed by habit or learning).

Not progredience (which is a spurting or leaping). Not progress or progressiveness (which is a capitalization of the past).

A de-regression. That's something *more unforesee-able than progress.*

We have to play with repetition, unless we want to exempt ourselves from life. We have to play with pulsating life which simply repeats involuntarily. Which rises to the attack again as involuntarily as the heart's beating. As involuntarily as the breathing of the lungs.

*

A burning, concealed hatred brings human beings together. It founds social life, studding it with surprises. It fulfils that social life in cyclical civil war. Human history isn't linear. The time, first, of animal societies, then of tamed animal societies—that is to say, Neolithic time which gradually became historical time—is seasonal, circular, agricultural, festive and faithful—an annual round. Society in the most developed societies continues to be *annus*, *circulus*, *circulus vitiosus*.

The *regressus* that fascinates and damns it lies in this.

History is a vicious circle.

Human societies, derived imperceptibly from animal societies, are doomed to a cycle of predation and wintering—of war and respite from war—which is increasingly out of attunement with the linguistic, technical, mathematical, industrial, financial, linear temporality that humanity believes reflects its nature but that produces a rhythm by which it does not live.

CHAPTER 57

The Fear of Forebears

Fear of mice is the fear of forebears. There are 4,500 species of mammal.

The ancestral form of mammals is a kind of shrew that lived in the Eocene.

All creatures with breasts derive from a sort of tiny insectivorous rat that makes us scream the way we might at a witch jumping out or a ghost appearing.

We are screaming at the sight of our ancestor.

CHAPTER 58

Everything that seems beyond the possibility of return seems to have left the realm of threat and to present no danger. But when the violent return occurs, we are devastated in an instant. What no longer exists is mere nothingness, yet this surging back without preliminaries hits us with the force of a cyclone.

And we find ourselves naked at the bottom of the abyss, while nothing has emerged into the real except invisible time.

CHAPTER 59

Orpheus (1), Son of Oeagrus

Orpheus, the son of Oeagrus, was a singer. He added two strings to the lyre. His wife died on a tree-lined shore. He walked past two rocks. He went down into the Underworld to fetch her. She was called Eurydice.

He sang.

Hearing his singing, Hades and Persephone began to cry.

They tearfully agreed to his wife's returning to earth. They imposed just one condition—that he shouldn't look back (*ne flectat retro*) before he had left their realm and returned to the valleys of Avernus.

CHAPTER 60

Orpheus (2) Aornos

Like Izanagi, Orpheus turned around.

Et nunc manet in te . . . And now may there remain in you,

Orpheus, the sadness of having turned around . . .

Orpheus poena respectus . . .

Oh, the *sorrow of respect*, which is simply a turning around of the soul towards death.

*

To fetch Eurydice from the Underworld, Orpheus travelled through the Aornas pass.

A-ornos, in Greece, on the boundaries of life, refers to the place deserted by the birds.

Psychai (souls; literally, breaths) in Greece were thought of as birds.

*

In 1826, the young Patrick Branwell Brontë wrote: 'Mount Aornos is our Olympus. It is the home of the Genii and the lords of the Jibble Kumri.'

CHAPTER 61

Orpheus (3) Recapitulatio

Kingdom: animal

Phylum: vertebrate

Class: mammal

Order: primate

Sub-order: simians

Family: hominid

Genus: homo

Species: *Homo sapiens Linnaeus*

Sub-species: *Homo sapiens sapiens*

Subjectivity: none

*

The biosphere is an immense tree that seems dead because it has many more dead branches than its few living boughs.

Sparrows, shrimps, crystals and human beings are the rare survivors of an adventure that began at the dawning of the world's dawns and is as yet far from its noonday sun.

*

Three to 4 million years separate the slow emergence of human beings from the sudden outburst of art. For 350,000 years, Archanthropians buried, tended to and ochred their dead, and put flowers on their graves.

It is difficult to distinguish between the invention of death and the invention of the imagination.

The ancient Romans called the skulls of their dead *imagines*.

Homoeothermic animals dream.

They hallucinate what is missing.

Men dream less than tigers.

But as much as birds.

The darkness of the womb precedes the aerial light of the atmosphere.

That darkness precedes its linguistic opposition to the celestial night by which its time is measured.

There is a 'there is' that precedes itself in primal non-visibility.

Two sources of the invisible: (1) It is the sexual that secretes the invisible among viviparous creatures. (2) It is language that secretes the invisible among humans (everything that can be said in language is set free from what may be synchronous).

The involuntary dream figures first the unfigurable, then the absent.

Natural language represents the absent, then transports all of the figurable into the unfigurable.

*

The bone marrow favoured by vultures came to be the favourite food of men.

The honey favoured by bears came to be the favourite food of men.

Before the 'not so very long ago' of the times of human speech, caves were first, in the deep past—the Erstwhile—the lairs of the most fearsome wild beasts. The big cats lay in them. Bears hibernated in them. These were the models and the ancestors. They are among the figures represented on the cave walls, as are the denizens of the other world themselves, an other world which they both pre-occupy and defend.

Animals are not forgotten by dreams. They are more numerous in dreams than in the ordinary course and scope of our lives.

There is an Erstwhile more powerful than the past which language and memory make available to us.

*

Buffon wrote: 'The beasts are without signs that are accessible to us. To us their gaze remains an indecipherable language. One can only imagine that their silence, a silence broken by nothing other than their animal cries, expresses *the dumbfounding of all their senses as soon as they are disconcerted.*'

*

Hunting, as imitated predation, began 1.6 million years ago.

Man became omnivorous because he was a predator on predation. A *praedator* here means strange *imitator,* where identity is forgotten in the transfer from carrion-eaters, beneath the skins, antlers and feathers. Carrion-feeding is hardly represented at all: eagles, wolves, dogs, foxes, boars and human beings themselves do not loom out at us much from the cave walls. The quasi-selves are the figures almost absent from the images.

*

What I term the past is shorter than the Erstwhile.

The past is merely human.

A wandering that first begins to stray around 1 million BCE so far as the bare-skinned subspecies is concerned.

Carrion-eating after the fashion of birds and in imitation of hyenas around 800,000 BCE.

Simulated carnivorousness and collective hunting around 500,000 BCE.

Fire at 100,000 BCE and lifelong light, cave exploration, the crossing of the Bering Strait on foot, tombs, languages, marriages, gifts, circulation, sculptures and paintings.

Agricultural settlement and granaries date from 9,000 BCE, granaries leading to towns, prompting envy and theft, unleashing wars, kings, reckonings of moveable feasts, writing systems.

*

We shall never know when the perpetuation of dead men's names in the bodies of the newborn began—the transfer of identity, the name's moving from one person to another, the *phora*, the *meta-phora* of the qualities and sign of the ancestor, of whom the newborn is supposed to be the—seminal, genealogical—spitting image.

In 13,000 BCE, the last Ice Age came to an end.

The invention of tombs began. Men began to meddle in the world of bears, dispossessing them of their incubators, of their springtime cook pots.

These were underground caves with no daylight, nights when the sun failed to return—caves outside of external time.

Caverns where *old time dwelt.* Caverns from which the glaciers had withdrawn, letting the springs gush forth.

This was an outside-of-time from before time, a pocket of viviparous life and a source, an ante-solar before-time.

Men regarded the bears of the Ice Age as the preceding kind of man. They were giants who were masters of the ossuaries and of the scratchings on the walls; of honey, springtime and gushing waters; of salmon fishing and so on.

In 12,700 BCE, the average summer temperature rose suddenly by 15 degrees.

Forests grew. Europe became covered in birch trees. Then in pines. Deer, aurochs and bison appeared. In 9,000 BCE, oaks sprang up, with elms, hazel trees and cities. Catalhöyük in 6,000 BCE had a thousand houses with 5,000 people living in them; in each house, the main room was set aside for the 'kill'—for horns and skulls. Entrance was gained through the roof. Sea level (at -130 metres during the glaciations) rose to its current level (the level we call zero) around 4,000 BCE. In 3,500 BCE, the desertification of the Sahara began and 'modern' times—this is what is known as Antiquity. Modern times are defined by castration and domestication,

hunters become subjects,

wolves dogs,

aurochs cattle,

boars pigs.

*

In the Palaeolithic, the human mind was still populated by images—the souls of the hunters were obsessed with dream visions followed by figurings of animals painted on the walls of the nocturnal caves.

In the Neolithic, due to the growing circulation of signs within groups that were domesticating themselves in the way that plants, rivers, seasons and species were being domesticated, voices were hallucinated in the same way as those dreams had been. Temples of stone were raised for the voices to dwell in. Natural languages proliferated.

At the end of the ancient times of the Egyptians, Jews, Greeks, Romans and Christians, the hallucinogenic voices disappeared. Trances, omens, oracles, sibyls, demons and prophets went away. Consciousness emerged. The lost voices were written down in the ancestral languages; they were complied with in the form of codes and books. The last gods dictated their last books. Hallucinogenic subjectivity (the self is an inner hallucination that echoes the internalization of language) progressed to the point of the self-contemplation of internal space, individual time management, personal guilt, confession.

Suddenly, the domination of the mobile over the sedentary took the form of the strange new ranking of armed, mounted men above farmers on foot tilling the soil.

Animal husbandry on horseback, which was extremely unusual in human history, beginning in 2,800 BCE and ending in 1789. On the hillsides of Afghanistan in 2001, men on horseback were still to be seen fighting against aircraft.

CHAPTER 62

The Seven Circles of Zenchiku

When Zeami died in 1444, Zenchiku set about writing Noh plays that were darker than those his father-in-law had penned.

When Zenchiku died in 1470, he left behind this piece of writing: The hearts of the dead are strangling us. The language learnt from our fathers is like ivy growing up from the depths of the body. Seven circles there are in the world, into which humanity returns at fall of night and lies down in silence.

The wheel of the sky, which makes night and day, is unlimited in its longevity. This is the first circle.

Growth is the beginning of the circular movement itself. Spring drives that movement and it is the origin of everything. Such is the second circle, made of pregnant bellies and burgeoning buds.

Fulfilment—this is the circle of swelling summer.

Forms reaching their maturity constitute the fourth circle. They grow taller or open out in the autumn's harvests. They bend the branches of the trees as they come to fruition, and fall from those branches.

Decline is the fifth circle, hunger, waiting, images, daydreams, dreams that hollow out the body and believe they see growth, new shoots and hail them.

In six are the circles around the fires of winter, where bodies huddle together. Circles in which bodies get down on their knees, in which foreheads touch the ground; courtesies, venerations, refrains and rounds that bring things back again.

Seven is the circle—the tiniest, the lowest— wherein our origin lies; the drop of pale, white dew that spurts and falls, which has already disappeared from the silk trousers or the woman's dark, gleaming mane of hair. Every man is a drop of seed that mingles with the single wave of the time of the Erstwhile that returns endlessly.

CHAPTER 63

Eos

Long, long ago, it so happened that Eos invented the stars.

A hand whose fingers are still red with the flesh of the prey it tears apart—then rosy fingered when forgetting that or trying to forget it—opens a single door deep in the darkness of the caves and stays itself on the depths of night.

One day that hand surprised a young man sleeping, with his sex erect. Eos was immediately flooded with desire. She approached and whisked away the dreaming Tithonus.

Time passed. Tithonus became Cronus in the bed of the immortally young Aurora. His beard was growing white at a great rate.

Later, nascent Day carried the ageless Forebear in its arms.

In the end, tiny Dawn hung her dried-out husband on a branch in the garden, he, barely alive, having become an invisible cicada inside a cage.

*

One day at Troy, in the course of the fighting, Aurora lost her son Memnon. She went immediately to Zeus and said: 'I would prevent the night from crossing into my realm if you didn't grant me a pyre for Memnon. I want a pyre whose smoke will be *as black as the night into which he is going.*'

Zeus thought for a while, then granted her wish. It was from that day forward that the impenetrable smoke of the cremation of humans blocked out the daylight, intercepting the sun's rays on the morrow of their deaths.

*

If Dawn remembers the cicadas, if she spreads her dew before desiring human beings, Night remembers the dragonflies.

Dragonflies, which are older than the birds, saw the dinosaurs go by.

CHAPTER 64

When women we love are asleep, time is halted, the immemorial returns and something that is a stranger to time is near at hand. Something we knew ourselves in the long night—itself a purely instantaneous present moment that preceded the first day—is alongside us, half-open. What are the dreams of the ages? When we see a bow, when we see a viol, when we read Chinese, Sanskrit, Greek or Latin, what is there behind the enigmatic sounds of the ages?

The same present murmuring background, as distant from everyone, as ineffable for everyone as it is constantly accessible.

The same background of night that stands unfailingly behind the stars.

The 200-inch Hale telescope at Mount Palomar is less powerful than the simple past.

The colour black is more powerful than the aorist tense.

The darkness of the sky after the sun has gone down shows that the stars haven't always existed. The night sky says: 'The universe is young.' If the universe is young, then time is recent. The sky isn't so overpopulated with stars as the earth is with people. It isn't crammed with worlds.

It is crammed with nothing, black with emptiness.

Night is the background of the sky.

None of the figures that people the sky, as arbitrary or fantastical assemblages of stars, really belongs to the night.

They are signs that were read in the dark sky, hallucinated as irresistible images of hunters.

Signs of birds of prey. Signs of wild beasts, of bears projected on to the black emptiness.

Thus did the Erstwhile remain on the backcloth of the sky, in a space before the past.

*

In ancient China, just as breath gave life to the earth, so too books came down into the world.

They are anachronistic black-lettered forms of precipitation.

The world was the first book.

The sun, the first eye that read it.

Then came the shell of the tortoise, criss-crossing the seas and never knowing death. The ancient Chinese said: 'The tortoise poked its head out into this world

in the same way as the desiring member poked out from its sheath of skin,

as the child poked out crying from its mother's vulva.'

*

The primal is formless.

The primordial formlessness roams about the depths of the sky, frolics in the supreme origin between the different—and indifferent—signs of the constellations.

*

Everything verbal, linguistic, bookish, narcissistic, glittering, thought-out and conscious will always be strangely disproportionate by comparison with the formless black of night, with the viviparous half-darkness—with that hint of shade that runs along the riverbank and ends in the water by the nettles,

the water willows, the frogs and the stubble fields.

*

Having begun life as nocturnal creatures, mammals are attracted by caves, darkness and night to such an extent that they rebuild them, lie down, curl up and dream.

An immense night surrounds each hour the way its halo surrounds the moon.

Every light presupposes this more ancient night which it overcomes or rends asunder.

Among the earliest humanity, time was counted by nights. The cycles of time were based on the *noumenia* (the absence of any sign).

*

To the darkness of the vulva, then of the womb, then of the cave can be added the darkness of the throat, then the intestine. The darkness, the blackness of the internal. Anal darkness is almost recent. It is almost an inference.

Time as twilight Hour. The hour, as we say in French, between *chien* and *loup*—dog and wolf (between teeth and fangs, when we regress from domestic animal to wild one, from talking animal to dreamy starveling).

When man regresses from the Past to the Erstwhile.

*

Ancientness was equivalent to essence.

Projecting into the past was equivalent to providing a *raison d'être*.

Ab initio lends time a story and seems, in so doing, to establish and orient the unstable, the formless, the disordered, the confused, the unorientable. For time to have a meaning, the origin of time has to be invented. For the child to have a meaning and live, he needs his mother, then his mother's father, then the circle formed by the two semicircles of the two families, the forenames and the names, the language that binds together all that it differentiates.

In illo tempore is the colour of every story.

A nocturnal colour, a lunar colour, a *noumenia* colour (a non-colour; in the absence of the moon, it is the Lost One that is seen in the empty sky).

The idea of origin is a powerful drug that gives rise to images in the mind.

In every true work of art, this explosion explodes.

There is no dawn that rises without rending apart a nocturnal backcloth.

Everyone goes back in their minds—in the flash of *noesis* itself—to the primal scene, to the explosion of astral seed.

Plato, in *Menexenus* 238a, wrote: 'It is not the earth that imitated woman in the matter of conception and birth, but woman the earth.'

CHAPTER 67

It is far from easy to define the night. Perhaps we should simply say: It is human beings' terror. The fear which made them as they are, which preceded them, which they circumvented with ritual, which they deflected with their strictures, which they peopled with images. They were not imagining—as they contemplated the night, they were blocking the memory of the first world.

CHAPTER 68

Cur

As a child, my head was often 'miles away'—'on the moon', as we say in French. I would recover my wits only to find myself kneeling, as punishment, in the corner of the classroom. The moon is the place where the nocturnal Erstwhile ends up and is transformed. It is sexual reverie that does not yet know its name. The aorist is a toxin. The thinker carries in his hands—when those hands are empty, when they are bare, when he examines them—the primal why.

We are endlessly stubborn recruits to causes whose origins are shrouded in darkness.

I need mention only the addiction to the *cur infantilis*.

The question of the starting point is the most primal of questions.

But, before all whys, it is the 'question' that is 'primalness' itself—before the dawn, before birth.

There is nothing prior to beginning, just as there is no answer prior to questioning.

Nothing can control that which rends asunder.

Origo is a term of ancient astronomy.

The Latin word *origo* comes from *oriri*. *Oriri* referred to stars becoming visible. English says of the sun: It rises on the horizon. *Oriri* is closer to *surgere*— to well up.

The sun wells up.

This gives us being as *that which wells up everywhere*.

The place of *oriri* is called the *orient*.

*

The true questioner is always opening up; is always making things well up, rise up, surge up; is always tearing things apart, opening the two edges of the wound, parting the two lips of the question, separating the two sexes of sexuation.

Is always pulling apart the two poles of the relation.

Is always differentiating anew, endlessly, ceaselessly, without boundary or horizon.

*

One should never answer.

There is something unimaginable beneath every image.

The *substrata* reproduce what we were when we were in the *placenta*.

A strange relation.

Let's take images of the pre-imaginary of one body enfolded within the other—like the enthusiast enfolded in his passion. Like the reader enfolded in his reading. Or his passion within the mother.

CHAPTER 69

Endymion of Elis

It so happened that Endymion of Elis fell asleep in the ditch beside a field. He dreamt.

On that occasion it wasn't the dawn but the moon that saw his erect member, desired it, drew near, straddled him and filled herself with his joy.

At the end of the night, the moon, seeing him wake, whispered that she would grant him a wish. He said: 'An endless, dreamless night, without you, beneath the dark sky.'

*

In the course of each day, colours become worn and their hues fade. So they invented the night, in which they merge and their differences disappear, as a time of recovery until dawn reappears and, with its blood, infuses new colour into them.

The way blocks of solid lava, crushed and pulverized at the centre of the earth, wait to recover all their erstwhile violence in an unpredictable, eruptive deflagration.

*

In the fifth century, baptism among Christians was a collective, annual event. After forty days of fasting and sexual continence, it took place during Easter night when neophytes were stripped bare and totally immersed in water.

Not until the end of the Middle Ages did Christians stop holding weddings at night.

CHAPTER 70

Where easel painting is concerned, the oldest *vanitas* dates from 1449. It is a skull set beside a broken brick.

The light is intense, almost lunar, and seems magical.

The background is black.

Behind the skull lies impenetrable night.

The death's head is what the ancient Romans called an image.

The painting in question is by Rogier van der Weyden.

Black bespeaks night (by night, Rogier van der Weyden understands the regular disappearance the sun undergoes).

The skull bespeaks death (by death, Rogier van der Weyden understands the disappearance that affects sexed living beings).

The broken brick bespeaks time (by time, Rogier van der Weyden understands the break inflicted on being).

CHAPTER 71

Nature isn't as old as time. It is time using life to make itself into a world.

The myths of modern science relate that 65 million years ago fire spread over a large part of the land, putting an apocalyptic end to the dinosaurs. Lemuriform primates were offered a piece of *palaeontological* good fortune. To be small, mobile and cave-dwelling were all pieces of good luck. Success went to those who could escape—into refuges that were initially crevices in the rocks. We are those who derive from those who could live in the night of the womb. A species that loves the shelter of great stones. We are the offspring of the offspring of the tiny lemuriforms. All mammals are post-lemuriforms. Those who are the baskets of their eggs. Those who are the houses of their eggs. The *Uterini*. The dwellers-in-houses.

The Erstwhile isn't the past. The Erstwhile is formless, indefinite, infinite, immense, aoristic. It is time immemorial—it is, as we say in French, *la nuit des temps*, the night of the ages.

Night here means a boundless milieu in which there is no perception.

Astrophysicist is the name we give to the prehistorians who are eager to see the past 'live'. Light moves in time. Perception itself is a fossil remnant of all that is visible. The telescope travels back in time and attempts to see the simple past through its lens.

But their vision is of time gone by.

The sky we gaze upon at night is not the sky of now; its heavenly bodies aren't present, its stars aren't contemporary. We are looking at a sky that has already been gone for such a long time—that was gone before we were here to see it.

CHAPTER 72

The Darkened

There is something of a stainless quality about folk tales that I suddenly find increasingly attractive. Something that leads me to abandon the novel to go back to an older, less human, more dreamlike, more natural form—to something quicker in the mouth and readier in the mind, something more thrilling.

Something that cannot age, or be oriented in space; something pulsational, spasmodic, short, imagistic, concise, dark, dense, spurting, and nourishing too, enigmatic.

*

At what point did the exoworld form the desire to tuck in its feet and curl up in the endoworld? Why do we need to disconnect ourselves from the atmospheric world so frequently? We wrap ourselves up in the old half-darkness. In some realm or other, we hollow out a non-existent space where we go to dream.

*

Melatonin, a hormone secreted by the night, is an old clock that marks not only the alternation between night and day but also that between winter and summer, coitus and reproduction.

*

For each of our bodies, the Erstwhile is situated in the little crumpled origin hidden between everyone's legs.

The Erstwhile for primal sexuality is that from which sexuation derives, from which fissiparousness derives, from which pulsation derives, from which acceleration derives, from which effusion derives—the first phase of time, with the astral explosion as the second phase. Excess roves around in the depths of the world. There is a 'dark', dizzying, purely 'questioning' colour before white and black.

In the 'darkened' face of time there is a little of the divine visage.

A little of the face of nowhere.

Of the shapeless face.

The night will always be older than the star that interrupts it.

There is an Erstwhile where the past flows that is not to be found in the past.

CHAPTER 73

Anaxagoras referred to the sky as his fatherland. The uranopolitan.

Democritus referred to the *kosmos* as his fatherland. The cosmopolitan.

Epictetus said that every man is unexilable. Statelessness is man's condition.

Plutarch said that the night is the only horizon I see. Our only house is maternal. We would perish if we returned to it. Our only country is the lost one.

CHAPTER 74

The One Whom Time Will Never Destroy

Vaster and vaster the One whom the course of time will
never exterminate,

whom time enhances,

whom no change changes,

whom otherness enhances,

whose face, maw, gaping jaws, harrowing cry, teeth
cannot be turned away,

Nor his magnificent necklaces of ivory, tusks,
horns, antlers, coloured feathers, white teeth,

Which open, eliminate, grind, crush, devour and
pre-digest, which dream, which speak as they dream,
which unfold in images that loom up,

whose decease is access,

whom nothingness magnifies,

whom sexual reproduction enlarges,

whom the ruin of cities enlarges,

whom individual deaths enlarge one by one,

who regurgitates them endlessly in the words of the languages of men,

O Past!

CHAPTER 75

God Become Past

The retrospective obsession is an ontological curiosity peculiar to the old Europe.

Archaeology is a European invention.

The accumulation of knowledge and of ages, etymology—particularly, the reconstructions of ancient European languages—palaeontology and Darwinism and psychoanalysis, plunging human beings back into zoological evolution and into the thrust of phylogenesis, have reworked our understanding of the globally primal.

In societies (even more than within individual men and women), the past always tends to resurface.

What every society fears (the dissociation of the *socius*) is the possible. This point haunts the collective media, which keep the refrains going that are sung to reassure the group and unite it. What every community is anxious about is the collapse of all trade and markets, civil war between all families, genocidal struggle between all groups, epidemics hitting collective sexual reproduction, an apocalypse in the world of values and gods.

As for the past, all European societies approach it either as folklore or as fossil. The Catholic religion, classical or baroque or Renaissance or medieval music, Athenian democracy, the Roman republic, provincial rebellions, highway robbers, brigands of the mountains and plains, public licentiousness, dialects and recipes.

The boundaries that protected ancient societies are only beginning to break down, with the beginnings of effects on all the divides of the past.

*

Up to this point, every human society has viewed itself as the reproduction of itself through a sacrifice. The rebirth of the hunting community by way of a spectacular killing. History doesn't like evolution, but it adores revolution, Terror, the repetition of any experience stronger than the present, in which reproduction seems to it to be slackening or rarefying. It always prefers the infamy committed in the past to daily life with its hope-sapping images. It mistakes the worse for the more intense. It is that other time when worse things happened. Societies' passions lean towards what they used to know, and towards what dazzled them within that experience. Towards what stirred humanity and forever defined its mode of life—lethal predation and cruelty imitated from the wild beasts.

*

So greatly did they fear the revenge of the wild beasts, whose tastes, appearance, predation, cunning and destruction they had imitated, and so ashamed were they of their animal origins that human beings massacred all the world's zoological animals on an enormous scale.

In some cases, there was total extermination.

In most instances, the population was reduced to specimens in collections or for breeding.

Humanity has removed a great many species from the conditions imposed on them by nature, the conditions in which life had spawned them.

CHAPTER 76

Louis Cordesse dealt in them. He was my friend. He had the same dark eyes. Eyes like the eyes of fossilized fish caught in naphtha.

Fins, strings of vertebrae, little bones from the head, and black eyes that had gradually become mineralized.

These fish lived in waters that were alive. This was long before human beings, long before dinosaurs, long before flowers.

Flooding asphyxiated them.

Then, as they dried out, they were left immobilized in silt.

*

Motionless, they embarked on another, more mysterious swim. They swam through time.

What enshrouded them will not enshroud our bones.

*

The fossilized fish imprisoned time more effectively than the ruins of Angkor Wat or Carthage.

We haven't petrified the world we have contemplated. These stones—or, rather, these petrified objects—that Louis sought to trade in, so that he could continue to paint freely, were of a substance that is more of our own day than the pages evoking Achilles, Gilgamesh or Amenhotep.

CHAPTER 77

On the Depth of Time

God became the past.

The depth of prehistoric time is something very new.

In 1861, Édouard Lartet managed to persuade the scientific community that humanity was antediluvian; that the current bodies of women and men were contemporary with animal species that had disappeared.

Lartet said: Our fears date from the time of bears in caves, of mammoths and aurochs.

The first Prehistoric Congress was held at Périgueux in 1906.

The vast extent of the past came as a bolt from the blue, as a volcanic, disruptive event—as something unimaginable to the whole of the human species over the preceding hundred millennia.

*

The past is an event that is, in some respects, *apocalyptic*.

*

The repeated discovery of ancient caves over the twentieth century can be seen as going back to the Second World War. Lascaux was discovered on 12 September 1940. It's true that dozens of these caves were found in the second half of the twentieth century because people were looking for them.

The abyss was hollowed out.

Excavations were begun in the cliffs and hills where they might be hidden.

But there's more than a strange coincidence in this.

A demand was met by a peculiar form of gift.

A meticulous dis-inhumation *after* so much involuntary incineration between 1933 and 1945.

An old humanity came looming up out of the humus *after* the inhumanity.

A new age was beginning, in which time and the past no longer had the same status, no longer had the same depth, no longer represented the same gift.

The dramatic irruption of the figurable on nocturnal walls came back into our world as the source of all—first dominant, then devastating—images.

*

From the fourteenth century onwards Europe began to dig. It was hell-bent on becoming its own antiquity. First through manuscripts, medals and statues. Then through buried cities and villas. Aqueducts and temples. Then pyramids. When their moment came, the Palaeolithic caves arrived on the site of Europe *as though they had been invented*.

Like the figures seen in the stars.

*

Libraries and museums took over from churches and palaces.

Sacred places where all the members of a group began to worship, gathering in silence around something neither-found-nor-lost (the *fascinus* of Osiris).

Societies that were increasingly religious and mythologizing, adoring themselves in the reflection of their past. Flocks of sheep, horned animals and dreams circulating endlessly around the empty, trans-temporal envelope.

*

In the great age of exploration, the whole of the known world became drenched in ecclesiastical Latin—a fact we might well find astonishing.

All the more astonishing, indeed, as Aramaic, Hebrew and Greek were all more likely to have been spoken in the houses of Yeshua than the tongue of the Romans, which was merely the persecutory language of the triumphal arches and crucifixions.

*

Why were the Vikings ensnared by the remnants of a dead language that lay entirely outside their history?

The Aztecs set about learning Latin.

The Chinese drew as much on Indian and foreign cultures as the Japanese pillaged the civilization of the Koreans and the trading posts on China's eastern seaboard. Japanese Buddhism, Chinese Buddhism and the Buddhism of the Indians have very little to do with one another, apart from the name of Buddha by which they are referred to generally. The bands of apes known as hominids derived the whole of their world from the self-interested, anxious examination of animal predation—stratagems, traps, customs, dances, languages, cultures, clothing. The first mode of imitation is devouring fascination.

Themistocles complained that the mind was never free of the past.

One day, a man from the city of Alexandria offered him a mnemonic device. He brushed it away with his hand and grabbed the man by the arm; he implored him, saying: 'Give me an art of forgetting.'

The man from Alexandria doesn't understand what is happening to him. In the agora, he wrests his arm from Themistocles' grip and steps away.

But then Themistocles crouches down; he caresses the Egyptian's member; he clings on to the Egyptian's knees; he implores: 'Bring me an art of forgetting!'

*

Charlemagne's Europe took over the theme of renascence from the Romans, who had meditated on it themselves when attempting to make anew the confederation of Greek city-states that had formed around the Acropolis of Athens.

The Europe of Venice and Florence did the same.

Charles V, Francis I of France, Napoleon, Mussolini and Hitler took up the theme.

I contrast the area of births with the area of dawns.

The groups of Inuit lived in discomfort for millennia. When explorers discovered them, they asked why they had stayed in such cold parts, in famine conditions, on that more-than-austere kind of ice bridge between Europe and America. They said: 'We followed the sun. We stopped in the place where its presence made a promise in the skies. We live amid our perennial prey, in the area of dawns, between the bears and the reindeer.'

The area of dawns—this is the name of the domain of the past.

*

When Engels and Marx read Lyell's *Antiquity of Man*, they were staggered by it. The sudden extension of the scale of human times left them reeling. With the immense dimensions now allotted to the human timescale, very slow changes could be envisaged, involving periods almost infinite in duration. The formation of the sky, the sea and the earth, the changing of forms and the development of species no longer had need of any external creation at their source. Neither external, nor divine, nor catastrophic.

Time itself was a sufficient provider.

The past had become so massive as to be self-generating.

The differentiation to which sexuality doomed the human species, the interbreeding and instability it involved, turned human history into one inexhaustible metamorphosis. That metamorphosis was constantly re-working the common core with the help of an otherness that never let things rest for a moment and had no overall purpose to it.

*

The past is a delicate product. It is extremely fresh, fragile and perishable; it dates from only yesterday and has barely made it out on to the surface of the earth.

The unprecedented development of prehistoric archaeology and of the anthropological research termed 'ethnology' have at a stroke reduced the domain of history by comparison with the depths of prehistory.

Archaeologists and ethnologists have definitively miniaturized the five civilizations that followed on from the four inventions of writing.

In regard to the forest of time, human history has acquired the appearance of a little bonsai pine watched over by three or four obsessional gods.

The past is a depth in which legend is but a single cry.

If we relate it to the whole of human experience, the Christian era is a mere lash fallen from the eye of time.

*

A suddenly immense Erstwhile.

Homo sapiens sapiens was a species that lived between a brief 'having-happened' and an even shorter 'yet-to-come'.

A yet-to-live even shorter than what has been lived.

The past was shared among the two or three preceding generations. It was limited to the names and forenames taken from those generations. The future was surviving-human-life. If possible, the ancestor handed on life and property to the descendant, who maintained the heritage and took over the patronymic. The object of life was to keep turning over what had previously been turned over: to bring back births, names, forenames, songs, tasks, springtimes, regrowths, appelations, prayers.

From the fourteenth century onwards in Europe, *Homo* became a suddenly dimensionless having-happened—*an immense memory*—made possible by the invention of the metric, technical referents of time.

An immense having-happened, in which the discoveries of primitive societies and distant civilizations were suddenly stacked up.

*

An immense having-happened into which the human species crumbled the primal position (the gate of the Erstwhile in the sky), polarizing itself on the basis of a progressive present. Inventing the present as a position of hatred of what was gone, the present as a position of exterminative future, the present as a position of credit, as a futurization of all moments (personal immortality, leisure, annual holidays, perpetual choices).

Two positions came into competition: the 'erstwhile' position and the 'credit' position (*credo*, belief).

Ancient human society—which took as its reference the return of what had come before, the 'erstwhile' position—saw only decadence in everything. It experienced time as the ruining of the primal. It imagined the 'Erstwhile' as an increasingly ghost-like returning presence. The absolute *senex*.

The monetary, explorer societies—which take as their reference the credit to be preserved and the investment of belief in profits to come—transform the real into a projected realization. All work becomes bearable on the basis of future life (the next holiday trip, the family's advancement, the children's education, the amassing of property or financial wealth). This is the absolute 'tomorrow' position. Absolute *puerilitas*.

Societies that see only progress to be made at any present time; that burst into laughter at the ridiculousness of the past within any present period.

Childhood—which had very little existence at all in ancient societies and then only in the mode of as yet wild, mettlesome animality and linguistic incompetence—wrested itself from the repetition of the old and became the great household divinity.

*

(1) The idea of decadence and the idea of progress are religious beliefs. (2) The invoking of the future is as wearisome and pointless as the recalling of the past. By way of compulsory schooling, states destined their populations to an obligatory future, enslaving childhood to obedience to times-to-come. Exterminatory hatred towards all *There-was* within What-is.

The murder of every Laius (of every father-king) at every crossroads of time.

And the murder of Labdakos in Laius.

And of Polydoros in Labdakos.

And of Cadmus in Polydoros.

And of the Dragon.

And of the Sphinx.

Dead souls doomed to the 'When-I'm-grown-up'.

CHAPTER 78

Chuang-Tzu's Bird

The more time went by, the more it was recorded. The more it became visible. Then time was perceived by speaking human beings as an entity among beings.

Suddenly, on the death of the Messiah, time contracted *like a tiger preparing to pounce* (1 Corinthians, 7:29).

Suddenly, after the dead of the twentieth century, time spread itself out, *like an eagle hovering above what is*.

This brings to mind Chuang-Tzu's bird. This is what the Chinese hermit termed its *unforeseeable span*.

For Saint Paul, when tomorrow came, the end could only be moments away. He had the impression of being able to reach out a finger and touch the end of time. Kneeling before one's lord, one could grasp the fringes of the mantle of history. One could begin to set the apocalypse in train (the movement by which time's veil would be removed).

For us, the apocalypse has already taken place. The veil has been lifted. The past has assumed its unimaginable dimensions as abyss.

The *origo ekstatikos* of vertiginous time.

*

We no longer bring the past to us as Albrecht Altdorfer did when he dressed Alexander in Danubian or Rhenish costume.

*

In the second half of the twentieth century, within the past it was its alterity, its otherness that came to be loved.

The past become *Alter*.

Then *Alter* become *Deus*.

*

We are doomed to the past as we are to the dawn, as we are to the conditions of our birth, to the gaze of woman who reproduces us all, to the smile of the mother and the model she points towards. Deep within us, something which is them is constantly seeking to please those who made us. They, similarly, exercise a seduction above and beyond the mere life they have launched into existence. This is how, through grandfathers slipping themselves into fathers, great-grandfathers into grandfathers, more remote ancestors into great-grandfathers, and fascinating gazes into those ancestors, the past seeks to supplant the erstwhile.

*

In the past, nature couldn't be called beautiful. For tens of millennia, it wasn't experienced as beautiful. Ancient humans would never have thought of simulating its image. Its authority and the fact of its existence, its terrifying fauna, its astral, meteorological, vegetal, animal domination and its ceaseless primacy surpassed the very idea of beauty. It was after countless cities conquered the earth and covered the available space with stone buildings and thoroughfares that natural beauty appeared—at a point when it was lost.

When loss transformed its face.

*

From the eighteenth century onwards, from the days of the revolutionary Terror, the bourgeois—the aristocrat too, and the rich farmer—built fake traditional buildings, fake classical ones, fake Pompeiian, fake

Gothic, fake rural. Even the modern is fake (a provoca-
tive fakery, a novelty that isn't spontaneous).

What I am writing here is one of the last indecipher-
ably scrawled texts that belong to an encyclopaedia—its
volumes numbered intermittently—for private use.

One of the last private registers of the kingdom—
a book to be put away in the right-hand drawer of the
sideboard of an old literary man who took the decision
to disappear off to his provincial retreat because this
world made no sense to him whatsoever.

To be truly scientific, from the twenty-first century
onwards, was to give up on subscribing to the primal
omnivorousness (even if omnivorousness, together
with metamorphosis, continues to be the underlying
reality).

I was at first surprised by this state of affairs in
everyone I met. My curiosity ran up everywhere against
heads secured behind high gates, heads that were
closed and had boundaries that proliferated, that hard-
ened, and walled themselves in.

Specialization has grown. The more precisely
defined a subject, the more limited the field, then the
more substantial international bibliographies on it
there are.

The *cura antiqua*—the ancient concern—is gone.

Science has become a moral entity, a distant, prohibitive, unreal thing that is no longer even conscious of what it is producing. There is nothing there to interest the Renaissance thinkers of the fifteenth century. Nothing for the encyclopaedists of the eighteenth. Nothing for Dante and nothing for Aquinas. Nothing for da Vinci. Knowledge is laid down piecemeal in the hard disks of the computers. These fragments are easily accessible and transmissible, but they neither short-circuit one another nor do they gather into a force of migrating desire to carry on, within their own particular essence, the roving quest itself.

CHAPTER 79

What is the abyss that is for ever at Pascal's side? The Seine viewed from the pont de Neuilly.

The Seine seen from the pont de Neuilly is the abyss. This is the baroque sensibility.

*

The sudden, total destruction of the possibility of anthropomorphy was the work of the free-thinking *libertins*, the Cartesians, the Spinozists, the serious, tragic Baroque of the French, the ecstatic, tearful Baroque of the English.

This was a melancholy more disconcerting for the Church than the neo-paganism of the late Renaissance.

*

When the Duc de la Rochefoucauld returned from exile and discovered the salon of Madame de Sablé, he initially saw it as the best way of getting close to Mme de Longueville again and to the son born of their adultery.

He had had no opportunity to see that son again since his exile. He embraced him.

He saw again the face of the woman who had been his abyss.

He had turned his suffering into a style.

He turned his return from exile into a game played with little pieces of paper covered with admissions, little savageries, pain and disenchantment.

Is there a crueller ordeal than a reunion with a former lover? The sudden barriers that come between you? The coldness? Or—amid all the politeness—a remnant of terrible anger?

He found Jacques Esprit now, like his former mistress, a Jansenist, and enticed him away from the duchesse de Longueville. He devoted himself to Mme de La Fayette. It was Mme de Sablé who gave him the chevalier Des Cartes' *Discourse on the Passions* to read.

It was Mme de Sablé's claim that she 'shone a lantern into the human heart'. That lantern was the rhetorical maxim, a thing passed from one person to another which everyone must work to perfect, in order to delve ever deeper into humanity's dark side.

As though there were a bottom to it.

La Rochefoucauld wrote to Mme de Sablé: 'The desire to write maxims can be caught like a cold.'

It was violence on an *epidemic* scale.

Which is still going on.

A persistent discomfort towards this *almost political fragmentation*.

The blood-soaked social bond, human love as the envious longing for everyone else's longings, complicity in pessimism, dark emulation and the struggle to find self-interest and bad faith in human feelings brought Esprit and La Rochefoucauld together until they were virtually indistinguishable. They understood each other implicitly, carrying on a wild insurrection with little bits of paper as violent as shards of sharpened stone.

CHAPTER 80

Modernity

The notion of *modernitas* appeared in the eleventh century.

The *Moderni* contrasted themselves with the *Antiqui* the way the Christians did with the Romans.

With each human life being regarded as a painful spell of time between Eden and Paradise, real life was transported into the third world. After the Ancients, the people of the origins and sin, Current Human Beings represented a median age, a Middle Age—*media aetas*—before the Reborn found new birth in an eternal future life.

So three progressive temporal stages, each more luminous than the last, each exterminating all 'Erstwhile', defined the human history of the Christians.

First there was the pagan darkness of the *Antiqui*.

Then the uncertain light of the earthly life of sinners, all of them tempted and almost all succumbing, most of them damned.

Then the full light of celestial paradise for the saved.

*

During the twelfth century—for the first time in social history—an abyssal historic distance came to be felt between forebears and descendants—the manuscripts the Christians had burnt were now brought back from the Byzantine and Arabic worlds. An abyss opened up between self and other, between ancients and moderns; people were staggered by its emergence.

A century later, Petrarch violently wrenched the notion of *media aetas* from its then meaning and plunged it into that abyss. The 'middle time' became a dark time of decadence, a chaotic, warlike, hostile time of vandalistic, gothic decay; with this, Petrarch contrasted the time of origins and its freshest, purest light. The Christian progressive timeline (pagan darkness, earthly half-darkness, paradisial splendour) gave way to a cyclical movement: childhood, old age, new childhood.

Origin, decay, rebirth.

Antiquity, Middle Ages, Renaissance.

*

The Renaissance was a pagan, republican, scholarly, bookish conspiracy. A cultural transmission that was no longer oral and childish but written and legendary, through exhumation among the Arabs and the Byzantines of what had escaped a deliberate, thousand-year annihilation by the Christians.

The Italian Renaissance in the fifteenth century was the finest moment of that anti-tyrannical, anti-Christian moment.

But the late twentieth century will have been the greatest period of renascence. The early twenty-first-century world found itself enhanced by a dizzying abyss of time, a wealth of knowledge and a—animal, biological, natural and celestial—heritage that was literally unimaginable in any other historical age.

The twentieth century's contribution was to hand on an infinite past.

The rendering-infinite of the past with the inventions of prehistory, ethnology, psychiatry and biology extended to the whole of the site (the earth in ruins).

The translation of almost all languages.

The synoptic viewing and the transmission of all available images.

The stockpiling of all the social experiences that can still be inventoried.

In the course of a century, in all the societies of the earth that have survived in terms of descendants and languages—themselves more or less synchronized through the *media* by which they intercommunicate—the time of private genealogy, the time of human history, the time of the chronology of nature, the time of the evolution of life, the time of matter, the time of the earth, the time of the stars and the time of the universe now form just one single leap.

*

An immense swathe of previous time which, *for the first time since the origin*, came at the question of inner human experience with the post-diluvian as starting-point.

*

Why will the past always be bigger than the future? The symmetry of the other world adds itself to the dynamic chain of actions and further joins to those the mythic but spontaneous chain-links of the pre-originary. The human world (which has only the child as its future) installs the other world (the genealogical, social, natural, animal, primal, stellar or mythical word) in the time before birth.

Birth is the only archaic dimension of time. It is the only date through which the searing afterwardsness of time emerges, ranging against each other within language the invisible past (the dead man) and the language-less future (the child). The only future is one of rebirth.

CHAPTER 81

Quintilian the Grammarian

Time can be asynchronous, just as death can.

Quintilian the Grammarian is saying so when he writes that 'All is not said.'

There is a lack in language—which invents time as much as it stretches the brain—which means that there will never be any completion to what is said. In the human capacity for saying (that is to say, in the countless, involuntary inventions of natural languages), there is a devastating and expressive power to which no speech that issues from these languages will ever be able to put the finishing touch. The ambition in every act of expression exceeds what has previously been expressed. The moderns have more models to draw on than the ancients. This is Yoshida Kenko's paradox. The most modern are the best placed and have the greatest opportunity, having the most carcasses to scavenge from.

*

To the latecomers goes the greatest depth of field.

To the latecomers goes the aoristic, aporetic, disoriented fragmentation of time.

*

Quintilian the Grammarian quoted Euripides: *Mellei, to theion d' esti toiouton phusei.*

He delays, for such is the nature of the divine.

Man, who is merely a deduction from hunting, watches and waits.

The god, which is merely a deduction from the wild beast, delays.

This is one of the originary scenes of the human structure of time.

Afterwardsness, delay, *re-gard*.

*

Quintilian the Grammarian said there had never in the entire history of humanity been happier ages than his own, for the gifts he received from the past were the most plentiful. The same goes for my own time if I compare it with Quintilian the Grammarian's and if I can compare myself with him. Each day the light grows harsher, but each day the golden age expands.

*

If an age is judged by the fruits it receives from previous seasons and from the sunshine that poured down into them, every season that begins is the finest there has been since the world began.

Every age is the most marvellous.

Every hour the profoundest.

Every book more silent.

Every past more lavish.

CHAPTER 82

Tautavel man, who went into the Caune de l'Arago cave in the French Pyrenees 450,000 years ago, came out again in 1971.

Given the incommensurability of human societies and natural languages, there is, for us humans, no unity to the past.

In linguistics, the zone of greatest divergence (of greatest dispersion) is called the oldest.

The most heterogeneous area is termed original.

*

The absurd measurement of the immeasurable. *For a little while now*, certain rocks on the earth have been more than 3.5 billion years old. The staggering clarity of a multiplicity beyond the bounds of memory. But being has not just been dispensed to us, human essents that we are. Perhaps it has been dispensed to something else entirely. Being has perhaps excommunicated man. In the depths of the heavens, 'light makes itself manifest' (Spinoza, *Ethica*, II, 43).[14] The transparency is such that no purchase can be gained on it. Incompatibility of *knowing* and *being*. Epochs are waterfalls and eras changes of riverbed to which rivers pay no mind and humans ascribe no meaning. The different worlds are totally unintelligible to one another and can never be put together in any single temporal location. We have to manufacture more powerful lenses than those which he polished. Hebrew was wrested from my mouth by the synagogue before everyone's eyes. I opt for a dead language and baptize myself *Bene-dictus*— well-said—devoting my life to that 'saying'. The substance of time is pure *alteritas*. Pure *evenit*. Everything happens. God is the *Asylum ignorantiae*. A single scattered pulsing passing through every barrier that helps it to appear and behind which it withdraws, because it tends to melt into it in the—itself radiant—light. But death is the proof that totality is not entire unto itself. That everything is ruptured, like sex or time.

*

It isn't just knowledge that has increased. The unknown also, in proportion.

All light surrounds the space it illuminates with the shadow it produces.

*

The abyss of 1945 says this: The species is not built the way it had dreamt it was; nor has it constructed itself the way it had pretended to.

There has been no return of humaneness into humanity because there is no humanity. Nothing will make good what used to be. Justice is unbelievable and comical. Suspension of the statute of limitations is an insult and a ghastly sarcasm. The world lacks past because of history. And it lacks Erstwhile because of the past.

*

The European twenty-first century is a thing of melancholy, knowing, as it does, for the first time, that humanity isn't special, that meaning is constructed, that truth is unknowable and nudity unrevealable.

An age of intense wonder where the excavation of the most distant things is concerned. The modern world is wrong to complain of the Unanswerability that has accompanied it—this is its extraordinary, eternally unpredictable good fortune.

Its sudden silence.

CHAPTER 83

The Traces of the Erstwhile

In ancient Japan, every man who had climaxed left a present behind as a souvenir in the room in which he had briefly spilled his seed.

Even if he had pleasured himself in solitary fashion—into his fingers—then after he had mopped up the drops, he left a ribbon, a card, a little roll of cloth or a fruit in the place, setting it on the floor.

I am thinking of an extremely thin man who chewed on liquorice root as he read.

I can see the long black dress that has been brought out for the bereavement that has just occurred in the Ardennes, on the edge of the forest, at Chooz—in the front yard, cousin Jeanne is violently beating with the wicker carpet-beater the material that hangs at the window;

the yellow sheet of the papyrus suddenly falling to the floor beside the Pleyel piano at Sèvres;

the full, yellow moon shining on the insomnia of a young man who is endlessly pacing up and down naked, from window to window, examining the black waters of the Seine that flow beneath the apartment on the Quai des Grands Augustins in Paris;

the voice of the stag coming from the mist-shrouded hill above the lacs de Boret;

two lovers putting their underwear back on and leaving each other in silence, on the brink of the chasm;

the leaking black boat beside the banks of the Yonne, still moored to its orange, rustproof chain, shipping water and sinking;

the absence of a cry of pain;

the nocturnal memory of a dead face;

the tearful face of a young German girl weeping.

CHAPTER 84

The Jagst

The acoustics on the river were so good that I suddenly heard the woodcutters, the jays and the longshoreman's cart, as though they were by my side.

*

The rays beating down from the sun are inexplicable. To our eyes, they are even more inexplicable than water.

The sun's rays are much more recent than our own bodies.

They have a marvellous violence to them. Curiously, after we are born, their presence calms us. But we do not see them—we are dazzled.

Their consistency, more intangible than that of water, is also stranger.

*

All along the rivers of Siam, Buddhist monks dressed in yellow glide in tiny boats. Their shaven heads glisten in the sun's light.

CHAPTER 85

Reading

In the late winter of 1945, Mohammed Ali el-Samman saddled his horse and went off to fetch some of that loose earth known as *sabakh*.[15]

When he drew near to Nag Hammadi in Jabel al-Tarif, he dismounted and began digging with a pickaxe around an enormous rock.

He hit upon something hollow.

He pulled out a tall red earthenware jar.

He raised his pick, brought it down on the jar and discovered thirteen leather-bound papyri. He got back on his horse and went off to sell them in al-Qasr.

CHAPTER 86

In Reading, the Eye Does Not See

Quod oculos non vidit, nec auris audivit, nec in cor homi-nis ascendit . . .[16]

What roves around endlessly within the soul,

What the word speaks of boundlessly,

What the eye has not seen,

What the ear has not heard,

What hasn't entered into the heart of man

Invades.

*

What the eye hasn't seen has invaded the heart through the man and woman that preceded that heart and made it.

What the ear has not heard poses questions in the—inexhaustible—acquired language but provides no answers.

ABYSSES

What has not entered into the heart of man invades us like an abyss.

CHAPTER 87

Antique Hunting

In the Trobriand Islands, reality is seen as aged, moth-eaten, worn-out, rotten. Only the Erstwhile is young. It is the origin of the gift. The birth of the land and the sea. The ancestral soul is mythic and the mythic is attested in traces—landscapes that the ancient narrative transfigures. These traces—mountains, springs, caves and shores—have captured forever the human experience that returns to them. Landscapes where magic operates, where the soul leaves the body when it sees them, the body falling silent or stock-still, or into ecstasy. Traces everyone journeys to, everyone returns to, everyone visits in order to identify them. Traces intensified by admiration.

*

We are elements of the universe. Our whole bodies bear the mark of this. And those marks increase in number as we live. The nakedness of our body, as it develops, holds in its memory something of the Erstwhile.

*

Chateaubriand's thrush in *Mémoires d'outre-tombe*, which has landed on the branch of a birch tree, is the Erstwhile in person.

Little primal, ancestral bird.

It is the bird on the stick in the well at Lascaux, beside the dead bison.

*

Abbé Breuil calculated that he had spent seven hundred days underground copying the images devised by the earliest human beings, in exactly the same way that a monastic copyist in medieval times would copy the traces of biblical antiquity over those of Roman antiquity. He sat on sacks filled with bracken, unfurling sheets of rice paper that he used in his tracing. His nostrils were blackened by inhaling vapours from the acetylene lamp that a young associate held up beside him.

*

Time is a consuming fire.

Ignis consumens.

God is an acetylene lamp.

It is possible that Dr Freud's passion for archaeology exceeded that of abbé Breuil.

They believed in a revelation older than books.

The Eternal spoke in images and the abbés and the doctors were their archivists.

They discovered the traces of an *abyssal Revelation*.

*

I went hunting for antiques.

*

We are gaining an ever-deeper understanding of the trace left by the past within the past and we find some strange orientations there; we are adding an enigmatic element. We are adding unpredictability to the 'It was' of all that was.

*

Cicero lost his daughter Tullia, who died giving birth at Tusculum. She was thirty-one years old. It was cold, since he says that snow had fallen on Tusculum. This took place in February 45 BCE. Everyone knew of the consul's passionate affection for his daughter.

Caesar, Brutus, Lucceius and Dolabella wrote to him.

Sulpicius, who was governor of Greece at the time, also sent him a letter of condolences which contains an argument that had never previously been employed.

At least, it was entirely novel so far as the Etrusco-Roman world was concerned.

This first melancholy trace in our civilization dates from 45 BCE.

(More precisely, Servius Sulpicius's letter is dated May 708 BCE.)

Sulpicius to Cicero:

I have to add a thought which recently consoled me. Perhaps it will be able to mitigate your affliction. On my last return from Asia, as I was sailing from Aegina to Megara, I was standing on deck and looking at the sea around me. Megara was in front of me, Aegina behind, Piraeus on the right and Corinth on the left. I said to myself: Alas, these walls once protected flourishing societies. Now they are, sadly, mere ruins scattered on the ground, gradually being buried under their own dust. Alas, how dare we, short-lived and scrawny as we are, bewail the death of one of our own— nature having made our lives so short—when

at one single glance, over the sides of the ship,
we see the recumbent corpses of so many great
cities?

*

For humanity, cities are the sediment of the time their
societies invented.

Time deposits itself there and builds a landscape
of destruction in which the destruction does not end.

There arises an extraordinary, *quasi-human
upright stance*.

Ghosts of cities on the surface of the earth.

For me, Rome is the most 'city-ish' of all the cities
I've seen in the world.

To live and walk in Rome was a violently moving
experience each time I stayed there. The intense co-
presence of all the elements of distinct periods, even
when set side by side, forms a strange, scattered unity—
a unity that involves no rivalries, that is heterogeneous,
calming.

A strange *pax romana*.

A mosaic in which the coloured stones are
Palaeolithic, palafitte, Etruscan, republican, imperial,
baroque and fascist shards of time. Were a fly to look
down on Rome, it might venture the idea that there

had been a species on earth for which time could be a liveable space.

Pompeii is the 'deadest town' of all dead towns, human death and its terror freezing the life of a town in a single instant.

With time leaving the negative images of the bodies there, as the life-or-death panic played itself out—those bodies the volcano reduced to ashes.

CHAPTER 88

Rhynia

There are mud casts of little settlements dating from the Bronze Age.

Wonderful things that lie, petrified, beneath the hideousness of the industrial suburb of Nola in Campania.

The plant rhynia, which stood one foot eight inches tall, owes its name to the place of its discovery near Rhynie, Aberdeenshire, where it was engulfed by a volcanic eruption.

There are flower Pompeiis.

CHAPTER 89

Rome

The illness of Pope Martin V afforded two men a period of leave. They wandered around the ruins. They put the young grey goats to flight that were grazing in the temples.

Without realizing it, and showing no concern to go back home to their families, they suddenly startle some hares which bound away. They are enjoying themselves.

Birds of prey soar up into the sky at their approach. The two men look up and observe the buzzards nesting at the top of the marble columns that are still standing.

They stand still.

At first the two men contemplate time.

Then they contemplate the sun.

*

One is called Antonio Loschi, the other Poggio Bracciolini.

The *De Varietate Fortunae* was written at the end of January 1431. The pope was to die, at Tusculum, on 20 February.

The two scholars, both employees of the Curia liberated unexpectedly from their duties, walk along the pretty little fast-flowing river running through the City, reach the island and climb the hill.

The sun is rising in the sky.

They clear away some brushwood. To decipher epigraphs on stones, they take their knives and clean the carved letters that are overgrown with moss or clogged with earth.

They eat eggs or drink fresh milk in a peasant's hut.

They wander around. In the distance they see the Pons Fabricius, the Arch of Lentulus, the Campus Martius and the Celimontano aqueduct.

They institute humanism. And they give a name to this fantasy. Poggio writes: *Urbe Roma in pristinam formam renascente.*

Renascente.

The city of Rome in its pristine beauty *being reborn.*

*

It is at this precise moment in his treatise—as the two are walking back down towards the sun as it sets amid the ruins and the vegetation—that Poggio adds to the fantasy of *renascentia* the hypothesis of *oblivio perpetua*.

He tells Loschi, 'We're speaking of the sites of places that have already passed from vision.'

Failure of memory is the Erstwhile itself in time.

'Everything sinks,' he says, 'towards eternal forgetting (*in oblivionem perpetuam*).'

This kind of abyss is in proportion to the Erstwhile that lies in rebirth, in *renaissance*.

*

Poggio to Loschi:

> I'm not one to forget days that are full of life and prefer the memory of shadows and slaughter to them. Though my full attention is on the ruins of time scattered about the space we're walking in, I don't hold the men of the present inferior to those who went before them. They're buffeted by this wind of death and uncertainty that arises from the depths of time, yet not only suffer it with the same bravery and fortitude, but also—in addition to

the identical or comparable bravery and strength—with the increased sense of grief that comes from the ever greater burden of the accumulating past.

CHAPTER 90

Virgil

They move forward cautiously amid the long shadows, the brambles and the patches of golden light from the setting sun.

Loschi quotes Virgil: 'Now golden, once bristling with woodland thickets.'[17]

Poggio: 'Why does the world collapse? Why is space undermined by the time that unfurls it?'

Poggio is the increasingly abyssal grief that each Renaissance conceals.

*

The shadows spread to their legs, moving up towards their genitals hidden in velvet. Beauty is rising.

The sun is setting.

To Loschi Poggio points out the Aventine hill, which lies before them bathed in the last rays of the sun.

The rose-tinted Campo Boario.

CHAPTER 91

Red

Matter, in its depths, is red.

Everything within us remembers this. Every approach to the Garden causes us still to blush. Our sexual organs remember it. Our hearts remember it.

Shame suddenly abandons us to a colour 15 billion years old.

Ochre paints us with the colour of volcanoes.

A heterophagous colour in which air and oxygen mingle.

Time is older than space, and older than the stars that illuminate it.

The earth so recent; a little newborn, lit by a light *that comes from elsewhere* and gave rise to life.

*

You seven little hills,

    once bristling with woodland thickets,

    hills that are so old and appear in a golden light,

    tiny mountains, crumbled into dust, dating from before the circle of the seasons,

    great recumbent animals older than the animals,

    a *problema* older than us,

    an *abyssus*, an animality older than us, a fauna older than form, a questioning older than the absent answer, a force older than life,

    an appearance always on the *qui-vive*,

    the point is not at all to 'deconstruct' the human temporal Ruins. Thinking is ecstatic. Thinking contemplates.

*

It is about contemplating unceasingly—contemplating more and more—the *Ruins arising* within their milieu, on their earth, in nature, on the surface of this savage, inhuman ground—ruins that are increasingly shattered and shattering, increasingly eroded and lost.

*

Freeing up the past of its repetition a little—this is the strange task to be performed.

Freeing ourselves not of the existence of the past but of its ties—this is the strange, meagre task to be performed.

Loosening a little the ties of what is past, the ties of what has passed, of what is passing—this is the simple task.

Loosening the ties a little.

TRANSLATOR'S NOTES

1 This would seem to be a paraphrase of the next two lines of Ovid's *Ars Amoris*: 'accedent questus, accedet amabile murmur, et dulces gemitus aptaque uerba ioco.'

2 *Les saisons et les phrases*. There is an echo here of *Les saisons et les jours* [literally, the seasons and the days], a well-known Prix Femina–winning novel of the 1930s by Caroline Miller, the original American title of which was *Lamb in his Bosom*.

3 The reference is to Lucius Aelius Stilo Preaconinus of Lanuvium, Varro's teacher.

4 Literally, everything happens.

5 Walter Pater, 'A Prince of Court Painters' in *Imaginary Portraits* (Rockville Maryland: Arc Manor, 2008), p. 23.

6 More 'traditional' readings of these Greek terms might give something like: Child playing-like-a-child playing draughts.

7 Pava is known today as Pawapuri.

8   The allusion is to Eurycleia.

9   'Qué bien sé yo la fonte que mane y corre, / aunque es de noche.' San Juan de la Cruz, 'La Fonte'.

10   In England, to which she fled as an *émigrée* and where her first novel was published, she is perhaps best known as Madame de Souza. She was, successively, Adélaïde-Marie-Émilie Filleul, Adélaïde Comtesse de Flahaut de la Billarderie and Adélaïde de Souza.

11   Missy was the pseudonym of Sophie Mathilde de Morny (1863–1944), who married the Marquis de Belbeuf in 1881 and divorced him in 1903. Her lesbian affair with the French novelist Colette created a scandal in Paris in the years preceding the First World War.

12   Jules Verne published *Voyages et aventures du capitaine Hatteras* (The Adventures of Captain Hatteras) in 1864. The character is thought by some to be based loosely on the English explorer John Franklin.

13   The Sanskrit drama *Vikrama and Urvasi* has it that a brazier of fire became the *sami* tree or *Mimosa suma*.

14   'Sicut lux se ipsam et tenebras manifestat' (as light makes manifest both itself and darkness). The Dutch philosopher Baruch (or Benedict de) Spinoza famously worked as a lens grinder. He was of Sephardic Jewish descent.

15   This is collected for use as a natural fertilizer.

16 These lines are from 1 Corinthians 2:9. 'Eye hath not seen, nor ear heard, neither have entered into the heart of man . . .'

17 'Aurea nunc, olim siluestribus horrida dumis.' Virgil, *Aeneid,* Book 8, 348.

TRANSLATOR'S ACKNOWLEDGEMENT

I should like to thank Leslie Hill, emeritus professor of French studies at the University of Warwick, for so generously giving of his time to discuss the work of Pascal Quignard and aspects of this particular translation. Thanks are also due to Marie-Dominique Maison. The responsibility for any shortcomings in the present volume is, of course, wholly mine.

286